T0151840

```
S A T O R
A R E P O
T E N E T
O P E R A
R O T A S
```

Copyright © Mark Gluth
2014

First edition

Sator Press
Santa Fe, NM
& Los Angeles, CA
satorpress.com

•

Cover art by J. Paige Heinen
Cover & interior design by Ken Baumann
Cover & interior font: Adobe Garamond Pro

•

No Other is a piece of music by Grouper.
The Idiot Sun is a piece of music by Leviathan.
Fake July is a piece of music by Gowns.
Reach For The Dead is a piece of music by Boards of Canada.
Spem In Alium is a piece of music by Thomas Tallis.

The epigraph from Part One is from *The Road*.
The epigraph from Part Two is from *Good Morning, Midnight*.
The epigraph from Part Three is from *Pattern Recognition*.
The epigraph from Part Four is from *Meditations*.

No Other

a novel

by Mark Gluth

Sincerest thanks to Barbara and Edward Gluth, Connie and Jim Kelly, David Hatch, Dennis Cooper, Derek McCormack, Diarmuid Hester, Habiba Sial, Holly Wilson, J. Paige Heinen, James Greer, Jeff Jackson, Jesse Hudson, Jonathan Arras, and Ken Baumann.

I miss you Dad.
I miss you Pearl.

For Erin Kelly

PART ONE:
THE IDIOT SUN

If you died I would want to die too.
– Cormac McCarthy

Summer

Hague was just there, or barely. The packed dirt was damp in the shade of the tires. It soaked through his jeans then underwear. Beyond it this field was baked and flat. It was the sunlight that was everywhere. The cone or whatever he was in was cool considering. This playground was what it was part of. It was this ersatz junkyard attached to the school that was the building that just loomed there. Hague heard a train in the distance. He pictured it. It disappeared when he shook his head. His headache didn't. It didn't matter. The opening over his head was blue. It moved way too slow for him to be able to handle so he dug at the dirt at his knees with this stone. He didn't notice he was holding it until he did. The smooth point dented the ground. The stone was slimy and it slipped from his hand. He pressed it against his forehead after he picked it up. The dirt and crap stuck underneath his fingernails was what he felt. He punched at something, everything. His fist hit the wall of the stack of tires he was in. They were strapped together by bolts. The whole thing rang. It gave way to silence. A cloud gave way to the sun. His knuckle was cut. It'd scab if he left it alone. He licked at it. His tongue was numb. The world sounded like his ears ringing. It smelled like ozone and tar. When he pulled himself up the playground was empty. Swings swayed as heat washed over sliding boards, the tan school. Hague stood in the middle of the parking lot. He walked towards some cars. It was just the direction he was walking in. When he leaned forward he spun then vomited. It pooled all acid and bilious on the cracked cement. He wiped his face and nose with his hand. He looked up when he stood up. These kids in the street were on skateboards. Hague's mouth tasted horrible. He'd pulled something in his throat. A boy on a bike laughed and shouted. Hague's teeth ached. He looked away. One of the skaters landed a trick all blearily in his periphery. Hague closed his eyes and started walking home. He thought maybe he could make it, or not really.

Hague closed his drapes and rested his head on a can of juice. It was frozen from the freezer. He fell asleep. It was nothing. Usually he could do it whenever. When he woke up his room was still dark. He walked around the house. The hall didn't have any windows and he stood in it. He rubbed his hair in the dim. When he gagged it was the taste in his mouth he gagged on. He drank some water. It made the taste run down his throat. He looked for his sister. He thought *Tuesday's not home. That means... she hasn't come home yet?* There wasn't a way she would have left without waking him up had she come home. He repeated that thought in his head until there was no way he believed it. He walked down the hall and waited at a door. It was to his mother's bedroom. The handle resisted in his hand. He said *Karen.* He said *Mom.* The air was thick and silent. That meant whatever until he checked the driveway. He poured some dog food into a bowl. He walked outside and set it down. The sky was a screen. It was all faded spray from the sun. He walked inside, flicked the knob on the TV. It was static. He stood in the kitchen and opened the fridge then the cupboard. The stove smelled like it was burning while he made macaroni and cheese. He dumped ketchup on the mound on his plate. He walked around the house. When he got into the static it was because he didn't hear it until he forced himself to. He thought that meant that it was everywhere. It awed him. He got into the buzz he'd gotten because his headache had gone away. These strands of light spun until his eyes thus the world were just lit. He counted as the pukey flavor faded. Numbers rolled forward. He missed his mouth, looked down. What he saw was just this blob of macaroni and ketchup on the carpet. He pictured his mom freaking out, the horrible fucking aftermath that was bound to ensue. He pictured himself losing it like he'd last lost it. Hague saw himself sobbing as he clawed at Karen's screaming face. He stood there then. He wasn't shuddering, he was shaking. The kitchen was where he grabbed the paper towels and Windex. He sprayed, scuffed at the spot with his shoe. He told himself that she wouldn't turn on the light. He told himself that she'll be too drunk to notice. His thoughts about the carpet began to thin out. Hague hated himself because he couldn't handle anything. He hated himself because he wished that he didn't hate himself. His headache came back. It was everything. His bedroom door swung open. It was the world that was spinning. The door, it bounced until it closed. He lied down on his back. The ceiling wasn't invisible but he could pretend. He had all this nausea and pain. He worked on ignoring it. Everything exploded into sleep. He had this dream: his head still killed, Tuesday came into the room, she sat on his bed, he told her about the carpet, she told him that it'll all be ok, *Mom will never know*, when her long hair disappeared into shadows the shadows disappeared, he could only see her face then, orange hooded and glowing. When she felt his forehead he woke up. When he woke up he heard a sound. It was this other sound that had woken him up. His door opened. It was Tuesday then Henry. She had let the dog in. She told him not to tell mom. She asked him what was up. Henry rested his head on the mattress. Hague told her that he had been throwing up. He told her about his headache. Tuesday touched his forehead. He pet the dog's head. The dog licked at his mouth. Hague said that he was glad that she was home. He said that the house was so empty earlier. She leaned forward, hugged him. The light came on in the hall. It came under the door and showed on the wall. Something in his head stung his nose. Tuesday pressed the dog down. He crawled under the bed. She did this walk as she headed for the door. Hague could hear it in the floorboards. He knew that she knew it would make him smile if he could see it. He knew that's why she did it. Hague just lay there and put his hand down. The dog licked it as he closed his eyes. The voices outside the door didn't make any sense. It was because he couldn't hear them.

.

Tuesday walked down the street. She walked across town. It was warm. The sun showed on her face, on her wind run hair. Tree lawns gave way to parked cars. She walked beneath branches and stepped through their shade. The sky was just hills then clouds then sky. The air picked up as it came off the water. Stairs lead towards this park. The carnival was there and crowded. She watched lights flash. She watched them change. The carriages on the Ferris wheel swayed. It was them moving and nothing else. The world was small and shining. It was how the light showed against everything that wasn't light. Tuesday only saw Sebastian once she saw him. These colors showed on his hair and face and glasses. He looked down. He didn't see her. His eyes lit when he did. His lips overwhelmed her. Something washed over her until it overtook her. Tuesday just kissed the boy. It became night. They took off on this trail that lead towards the mountains that ringed the town on three sides. Tuesday saw off and into the distance. Hills and trees were just shapes then part of the dark. They felt gravel beneath their feet in the night. The trail followed a switchback. Light came from houses. Tuesday and Sebastian could see the water. It was this break in the trees. The town below them stretched towards the harbor. The sky was lit by it and the stars. They lay down then. She picked at the grass. She braided pieces. He tried to light a candle he'd pulled from the back pocket of his jeans.

He lit it then. He leaned back and rested on his elbows. When she climbed on top of him she closed her eyes. She rested her head on his chest. She smelled his rank pits, he got hard. She bit his neck. They lay there. She opened her eyes. His face was gone in the dark and stuff. She made out shapes. The stars in the distance were just light. She heard the wind but didn't feel it. It was the top of the trees, everything above them. She couldn't feel his hair until she touched it.

FALL

Hague knelt on his chair and Tuesday just sat there. His wrists pressed on peeling Formica. The Ouija board was just a drawing on a piece of paper but she had made it for him so it meant the world. There was this lens from a pair of glasses that they found. It's what they were using. Tuesday asked him what was up with his voice. He said it was like that when he woke up. He said his throat was all sore. Their fingers pressed on the lens until it looked for something like it was there. The words were garbage but he wrote them down anyway. The table was sticky, everything that touched it. His stomach growled. He guzzled pop from a cup. Tuesday said *Hey kid*. She said *Slow down.* He kicked the base of the table, chewed on his cuticle. Tuesday looked at her watch. She said she had to go. *There's burritos in the freezer.* He asked her something. He didn't answer him so she repeated it. *Where's mom?* Tuesday told him she'd be home sometime. In his head he begged her not to leave. He said *You know,* he paused, he said *You know I can't handle it when she comes home drunk.* Tuesday said she knew. She said *I know kid.* She told him to just stay in his room, *It'll be ok then.* He sat there after she walked out of the kitchen. She said *I'll be out late k?* She told him she would probably crash at Kyle's. She was in her room. He thought that. He started talking. When she didn't come out he realized she was gone. He studied the paper, the pencil he wrote with. He flicked and spun the lens. When he focused he saw it clearly. It all faded though as his eyes ached with strain. They just got so wide then. Everything withdrew into brightness that bloomed till it overtook what had been there previous.

The leaves were changing. It was getting later sooner. Tuesday thought that. Out away from the water she wore a sweater and a hoodie. Sebastian walked up. There was this pond behind them. It was barely light enough to see it. She talked to him. She told him this truck gave her shit when she rode her bike out here. He hugged her. She breathed in when she pressed her face into his shoulder. Kyle's yard was huge compared to his house. It was a forest what with everything. Somebody passed around this bag of chips. The cooler smelled like fish but it was filled with ice. Sebastian got up to pee. He stumbled behind a dogwood. Tuesday watched until she couldn't see him. A tape was playing, or the radio. Tuesday hated the music but it was part of everything so whatever. That's what she thought. The fire rose. When she lay back her arm was a pillow in the grass. The lights that looked like stars were a ski resort, planes. Someone pulled a cap off a bottle of whisky that they'd pulled out of the ice. Sebastian lit a cigarette and lay back down. Tuesday was just there then. When she breathed in it smelled like soil and smoke. It smelled like wet leaves. The song changed. She knew what it would look like if her eyes were open so she kept them closed. Someone said her name. They touched her shoulder. Meghan said hey. She sat with her legs crossed, smiled. The shadows from the fire hooded her face. When she turned the light lit her eyes. Tuesday rolled on her back. Meghan said that she was so drunk. She said *Don't you just love it.* She lay down, rolled over. There were leaves in her hair, an earwig in her curls. Tuesday flicked it with a twig. It looked like it was gone then.

Hague was outside and the gravel hurt his bare feet but it was also the cold. The car was Karen's and he knelt down at the rear bumper. Henry was asleep there. The dog was resting his head against the right tire. His eyes were open but that didn't mean that he saw anything. Hague did the same thing sometimes. The dog's ear pricked because his bowl made this sound when Hague set it down. He said *Come on Hen.* He slapped his leg. The dog just lay there. Hague just left the food. He walked towards the back porch. Inside the empty kitchen was warm. The cupboards were tacky from grease. He heard a car pull up. He glanced around the shade. His mom was getting out of the cab parked in their driveway. He just grabbed some crackers and decamped to his room. He walked over to his bed, pulled the covers over his head. It was dark but he could see that it was dark. He was just thinking. *If the moon was dark and the night was white,* that's what he was thinking. What he was thinking was that those were just thoughts that he was thinking. It dissolved into sleep. There was pounding at his door, more. It wasn't dark which meant it was light. His mother's voice said his name. She poured him cereal. He knocked at Tuesday's door. *She's god knows where.* Karen said that. Hague said she's at Kyle's. He said that he was just checking. Hague stood in the bathroom then and pressed his hair down with water. Outside it was warmer than it was in the house. He dragged his bag through a puddle. The leaves blew all wild in the sun. He waited for the bus. He rode it across town. School was this bland wash until his last class ended. He skipped the queued buses. He took off to the library pronto. It was because there was no way he was going home until he had to. His stomach ached and his hands shook because he was hungry. He found a cough drop in his backpack. He unwrapped it. He cracked it with his teeth. The library was one big room and basically empty. He sat at this cubicle between the stacks and a wall. The fluorescent lights killed his eyes. That's why his face was in his arms. Some sound woke him up. He grabbed his stuff. He booked. It was dark and clear thus cold. The sky looked complex because the stars weren't hidden. His mind ran laps around that thought until it was whittled down to something he just knew. Whenever he thought like that he didn't see even though he could. He blinked. It was still the same. Hague ran towards a bus shelter. His ears got so cold as he waited. The bus was all glary. The lights wouldn't shut off. The driver was whatever about it. Hague's glasses were filthy and he could see it. At home he checked Tuesday's room. He brushed his teeth and fed Henry. The dog was so excited. He tried to jump up. Hague sat there in the driveway and hugged him. Henry limped in circles and tangled his chain. It wasn't his paw that hurt but it looked like it. Hague unhooked him and they jogged laps. He couldn't see him but he knew where he was. He kept running but the dog didn't. He got him water. He went inside when he saw lights coming down the street. His room was bright and stuff was loud. What he heard was tires as they skidded on gravel, a door as it slammed on ragged hinges. It was the thin walls when he heard her fall and start moaning. The living room lit after he turned on a lamp. Karen mumbled all sprawled such as she was. She said *Oh my god Haguey.* She was laid out with her arms stretched and her eyes shut. Hague thought it sounded like her mouth was full of shit. She yelled at him. He asked her if she was ok. He asked her how she drove if she was that drunk. She drooled, lay on her side. She said *Help me get up, just fucking.* When he leaned forward she grabbed his wrists. Her weight pulled on him. It was him being thin as shit that was the problem. Something slipped and she was back on her back. His balance was off and he fell forward. It was his brow that hit the coffee table's edge. He heard it as it happened. Karen yelped. He was kneeling, reeling. He touched his head where it hurt. His skin peeled back. Something stuck to his brow. Her voice was this dull hum beneath the ringing in his ears. What she said was that she was worried that she had really hurt herself. He began to stand up. He was dizzy and nauseous. When she braced her hand beneath herself she looked at him. He saw through the blood running into his eyes. She was just this shape he made out then spat at.

The light was blue in the rain then snow. The trees showed where it came from. Tuesday left her bike on the porch. She ran inside and peed. She lay down on the floor in Hague's room then. He was on the bed. She looked at the closed window. The ceiling fan was caked with cobwebs. She sat with her back against the dresser. Dusty air blew through her fingers when she rested her hand on the vent. She handed Hague a cup of cocoa. It was cold. He asked her what it was like outside. He asked her if she checked on Henry. She asked him how he felt as she checked the Band-Aid on his forehead. It was a thermometer she handed him when she said it looked like he was healing. He mumbled because of it. She told him to stop talking. She told him to close his mouth. The phone rang. The thermometer beeped. She said *Cool.* She pressed a

button on the phone. *Word is you're getting better, kid.*
Tuesday kneeled when she spoke. She got up, poured him
some juice. She left the carton on his dresser. She told
him she was going out. *No, it will be ok. There's milk and
cereal.* She stood in the hallway and wrapped her scarf
around the buttoned collar of her pea coat. She shoved
her hands in her pocket once she was outside. The light
faded fast and the temperature dropped thus. Downtown
was a run of lights down the hill that all the streets ran
down. Streetlamps showed on side streets. She pulled her
beret over her ears, waved at Sebastian from a ways off.
She pressed her face into his coat and just held it there.
They took off then. They cut down to the bay. Tuesday
looked at the sky over the refinery. When she said stel-
lar she meant starlike. The snow picked up. Drifts rose
behind them. They walked on the berm. Tuesday's socks
were cold and wet inside her boots. The snow was dusty
then and the wind swept it across the road. Headlights
showed the ground when cars passed. Sebastian stuck out
his thumb. The drivers ignored them, or they were blind.
The kids walked in the dark alone. They heard their foot-
steps and the snow falling and then silence. Tuesday made

27

out snow fencing. It was the field that they came through. They hit this cross street and turned. Streetlamps showed houses and sidewalks. A driveway wound up and around these trees and rocks. The house they saw was enormous. The door sounded like music. Inside, a girl hugged Tuesday. She ran her fingers through her hair. Tuesday said *Oh my god, it's warm.* She asked her where the bathroom was. The girl said she'd take her. She said she had to pee too. Tuesday looked in the mirror. She messed with her bangs. The girl wadded some toilet paper, pulled down her dress. She washed her hands as Tuesday pulled down her jeans and panties together. The girl said *Tuesday, your hair looks cute.* The seat was warm. Tuesday rolled her eyes, she smiled at her. The girls walked out of there together. When Tuesday walked into the kitchen Sebastian handed her a glass of whisky. There were all these candles and the house smelled like them. She bummed a cigarette. Sebastian rested his head on her shoulder. He held a beer, he got her more whisky. She couldn't close her eyes because she got dizzy when she did. Someone turned off the lights. Everyone was in the room together. Sebastian talked to this guy. He lit some incense. They started to watch a movie.

This woman was on the screen and Tuesday saw it because the screen was there. An actor coughed. Sputum was fake blood. The walls were mirrors and that's what it dripped down. Tuesday shook her head. She closed her eyes. She heard talking and music. It was the movie, she thought. It was light when she woke up. Sebastian was flopped on the couch with her. This guy walked into the room. He put his face in his palms. The snow was icy and it sounded like rain when it hit the windows. Tuesday asked the guy for a ride. She shook Sebastian. They were quiet in the car. In her driveway the guy asked *What the fuck's wrong with that dog?* Henry was yelping at the windows, the foundation. Sebastian hugged Tuesday and kissed her neck and then she ran inside. She stood in the hallway and saw Karen lying on the floor. Karen's face was pressed against Hague's door. All Tuesday heard was Karen pounding it. She heard Karen stop. Karen said *I guess you don't want to eat breakfast Hague.* She pressed the carpet with her fingers. She said *God damn it.* She said she wanted to see his face, she said that she needed to.

WINTER

Hague lay in bed. The air moved against him. The window wasn't open, he didn't have to look. It was the broken furnace. He looked at the clock. He hadn't slept, period. The idea overwhelmed him. He thought he'd have time to walk to school if he left soon. He got dressed, grabbed his sweatshirt and scarf. He shoved his hands into his pockets as he walked across town via side streets in the quiet dawn. The dark gave but the cold didn't and the sky was a bright and beautiful thing that he squinted his eyes against because it just killed them. When he slipped it was on black ice. His wrist and hand killed because of how he fell. The schoolyard was empty, as was the building. He walked down unlit halls to a bathroom. Gravel ran down the drain as he ran the faucet with his hand beneath it. He could feel his fingers. It was the hot water. The hallway smelled like chlorine when he left. A girl with wet hair pulled on a sweater in front of an open locker. Upstairs, Hague sat on a landing with his back on this railing. He gulped milk in the middle of the cafeteria. Banners fluttered beneath the vents along the wall. Glare busted off the windows, floors and tables. He left a note for Tuesday in her locker. He walked from class to class. When he looked into a microscope crystals bloomed. After classes he walked across the track. The sun hit the bleachers but he couldn't feel it. It was the air. He huddled and leaned with his hands in his sleeves. Tuesday walked out of the gym and towards him. He waved, she smiled. They walked home from the bus. She turned on the oven and they sat in the kitchen. Tuesday fixed spaghetti and they ate it on paper plates. She put towels in the dryer. They wrapped themselves while they watched TV. Its cold light warmed the boring living room. Tuesday walked into kitchen and cut a package of microwave popcorn open with a knife. She dumped it into a pan on the stove. Hague dipped each piece in ketchup. A trailer for this horror movie came on. It was set in a high school. This group of friends all played this satanic videogame. The game or something possessed them. They all committed suicide: one drove his car off a bridge; one fell on his sword in the woods. The screen showed a body hanging from a ceiling fan. It cut. It showed these cute kids staring like they were in a trance. Music rose and they closed their eyes. It was supposed to mean so much. Tuesday just sat there. Hague got up and out of there. Tuesday said his name. He heard it from beneath all the blankets he pulled over his head as he lay in bed. Everything was quiet because Tuesday had walked away from his door. Hague started to cry. He knew it was the not sleeping, the kids killing themselves in the trailer. He knew he couldn't handle it because of his father. Hague lifted his head from beneath the blankets so he could breathe. He wiped snot on his sleeve. The neighbor's porch light skirted beneath his drapes. It went away. Hague wrenched his eyes closed because shit was so overwhelming to him. He made a list of reasons to not commit suicide. He just started thinking it. The list was Tuesday and Henry. It was if Karen stopped drinking, if she started to love him. It was the off chance she would die and Tuesday and him could be orphans and happy. He thought that then. He just lay there. The next morning he wrote it down while he was slumped back in his seat on the bus. He turned it in for an assignment at school. A week later his teacher asked him to stay after class. She asked him to come with her. They walked down the hall. She glanced in an open door. They sat near a window. His teacher asked Hague why he had written what he turned in. She asked him when he wrote it. *Did you want these things to come true, did you think they would?* That's what she asked him. He looked at her then down. The room was quiet. He spoke then. She strained to hear his whisper. He started to cry. It was what he was saying. She reached for a box of Kleenex. He said it didn't matter. He said that it was ok. He wiped his nose on his sleeve while he spoke. He hung his head. She said his name. She asked him if he frequently felt, he couldn't hear what she said. It was his crying. She asked him if he frequently felt depressed. He picked up his feet and put them on the seat of his chair. He hugged his knees, buried his face in his thighs. When his head shook it was because his whole body did. It looked like the room was when he looked up. Everything spun into his vision. He was in the middle of a sentence. That's what she thought. He made this sound and then the chair did when he got up and kicked it back so that it hit the wall. His teacher stood up. She began to follow him. Hague dragged his bag like an anchor. Hague's teacher said *Hague.* He didn't turn around and she didn't catch up with him because she didn't try to. Outside, the sky was dim and white and everything was covered in snow. Plow built piles of the stuff banked the perimeter of the parking lot. It was gray and black from crap. Hague froze on the way home. Karen's car was in the driveway. She put out her cigarette when he walked into the kitchen. She told him that she should not have to talk to his teacher, that she should not need to deal with this bullshit. She told him that she told his god damn teacher that she was taking him back to that doctor, that she was going to get him back on that fucking medicine. Karen told Hague to not talk to his teacher. She told him not to say a fucking word. The woman stood next to the kitchen table and looked at the boy. He looked away. After his door slammed it was quiet in the house. Tuesday got home. She knocked on Hague's door. He said *Hey*, she left it at that. She found Karen asleep in the bathtub. She heated up frozen pizza and left the oven on. The air in the house felt stilted from whatever bad vibes poured down the walls. Tuesday drank coffee in her room. She looked at her homework. She put on a scarf over the sweatshirt that she'd put on over her sweater. There was a record playing because she had put it on. The songs sounded crushed, each of them. *Maybe it was because...* she thought that. Her thought fizzled. She couldn't focus. Things meant so much once she saw through them. She thought that with her eyes closed. It was as dark as it had been because her room was dark anyway. She heard this sound before she woke up. She ran into Hague's room, then climbed out the window and ran after him. The stars were nothing compared to the moon. It was dark because the moon was nothing to speak of. Her feet slipped. She watched Hague run down the street then across an easement. He stopped at the playground, cut towards these woods. She stayed back. She watched him as he stood. He rolled out his sleeping bag. She sat down on some leaves. She slouched back against a fence. He laid the blanket over some branches. It made a drippy tent. She shoved her hands in the front pockets of her jeans. Her nose ran, she laid her head back. When she opened her eyes it was lighter and colder and she walked over to the blanket hanging all lank against the breeze. She ran home and checked his room, the house. She shook Karen. She slapped her face. Tuesday screamed at her as she opened the blinds. She told Karen that it was her fucking fault. She said she had no idea what happened but she could just fucking tell. They called 911. Clouds got trapped between the water and the mountains. A storm set in. Karen kept calling the police. It was dark because the snow blocked the light. Tuesday walked out to the corner. The cold felt warm against her face. It was because she was getting used to it. She kept walking. The only cars she saw were trucks and the police. Karen smoked and paced. She drank coffee. It was 9 at night. Tuesday stood in the bathroom and sobbed. It was because she'd taken everything into consideration. It was 7 in the morning when she looked at the clock. It was because she'd heard the phone ring. Hague had been walking down some street a block away from the high school when the police found him. Tuesday and Karen rushed to the hospital. It was where they'd taken him. When Tuesday first saw him a nurse was rubbing a wash cloth over his face and lips. They looked different. Karen grabbed it away from the nurse and pushed her away. She scrubbed at the kid's face. He cried. His bangs got wetted down. His hair stuck up as she ran her fingers through it. Tuesday hugged him from behind. It was a bed that he was sitting on. Karen didn't stop telling Hague how much she loved him. She said *My baby.* He just sat there and leaned forward and bit the nails on his shaking fingers. When he looked up he wasn't looking. Karen brought him some hot chocolate and watched him drink it while he sat there. Outside it was bright because of the snow. Tuesday said *Hey kid.* He was the middle of everything and he was all she saw. It was his smile. He said that he was tired. He said he'd spent the storm in an abandoned car. Tuesday didn't ask him what the fuck was going on. She didn't ask him anything. There was this moment and everything was quiet in it. The hospital didn't keep him. His fluids were ok. He had this low grade fever. They told Karen to watch it. Karen got them a motel room because of the furnace. They ate McDonald's for dinner. Karen drank a diet Coke then water. They turned off the lights in the room and watched the snow as it fell outside the window. They turned on the TV. Hague kept changing the channel. He kept watching commercials. They fell asleep, then he did.

SPRING

Tuesday and Sebastian drank fast food coffee after school. They headed downtown then cut over a couple blocks. They jay walked, skirted along a river. It was a sludgy trickle, trash bedded in the banks. She put her arm through his as they tromped. The grey snow melted in the rain. The sky faded then darkened. It kept up. It was dusk and rainy and the world pulled through her. This path was a trail through the woods. Unmanned shopping carts stood outside unzipped tents. Thick mud stuck to their shoes as they cut through to his backyard. In his room they pulled off their soaked clothes. When he pulled her onto the bed he ran his fingers though her hair. She smiled, bit her lip. She laughed. He took off his watch. She piled her hair on top of her head. She held it in place then let go. He looked into her eyes until she shut them. They pulled the covers over their heads. They kissed. He leaned into her and she pressed against him. She worried about getting pregnant but the condom didn't look broken when he took it off. He lay there while she peed. The ajar door made the light make this line on the wall. She said she was jealous that he had his own bathroom. She pressed her forehead against his while they lay in bed. She wrapped her legs around his waist.

Hague pushed the shopping cart down the aisle. He slouched and leaned. He grabbed a package of cookies off the shelf. Karen told him ok. She broke a can of grape soda off the six pack in the bottom of the cart and handed it to him. The kid guzzled it, wiped the sticky corners of his mouth with the back of his hand. They stood at the checkout with the loaded cart. Hague tossed candy on the belt. He braced his feet on the cart frame. He rode it across the parking lot to the car. Karen loaded the groceries into the backseat and Hague stood there. Oil on a puddle formed rainbow colored shapes on the surface. Karen drove, Hague rode. *Do me a favor Haguey.* She had the kid turn around in his seat then. He rooted through the bags in the back seat. *No, not the whiskey, the beer.* He tore at the cardboard case. He handed her a can then wiped his hand on his shoulder. She cracked it then sipped on it. The road headed west and light from the setting sun came from behind the houses in front of them. Hague squinted because it was just glare, the windshield. They weren't moving. It was the red light. Karen asked him if he could reach her another natty. He looked at the dash clock. He kneeled on his seat as he faced backwards. He thought about going to school tomorrow. He thought about homework. He handed Karen the can. He said to her to make sure she doesn't get drunk. *You have to work tomorrow.*

SUMMER

Karen slapped Tuesday. She thought it was reasonable though she'd forgotten the reason. It was how drunk she was. Tuesday grabbed at her hair. They fell into the door. Someone screamed *You fucking bitch.* Hague couldn't tell who. It was because he'd watched them fight in the hall then ran into his room. It was because he was crying in there. When everything got quiet he realized he'd stopped. Something shook the wall. Karen screamed. It was at Tuesday. She said it was a rental. She said that they needed to fix it god damn it. Tuesday just walked away. She slammed the door. Karen moaned, uttered. She paced. In the kitchen she looked out the window. She walked out to the car. She pounded the hood after she couldn't open the locked door. There was that plus the way she was walking. Henry stood behind the car with his head all low. The dog snarled. She kicked him and he yelped. Hague ran out of his room and out the front door. He picked the dog up. He wavered like his legs were stilts. They made it to his room. Hague pressed his face into the dog's scruff. He closed his eyes and scrunched them closed until that and the smell of dog fur was everything. Henry walked behind him as he walked down the hall, into the kitchen. The dog stood there, whinnied then whined. Hague walked over to the cupboard, he grabbed a bowl. Karen was in the room then. She told him to get that fucking dog out of the god damned house. She smacked his face and knocked away the bowl. Water splashed, it sprayed. She grabbed the dog's collar. His head dented the wall. The dog stood up all spindly and blinded. Hague swung at her face like it was the last thing there was.

FALL

Hague lay in bed because his eyes and nose ran when he went outside. Karen was gone when he woke up and she'd been gone all the night before. He picked his nose, scraped at the caked crap that had dried all over his upper lip. The bathroom stank. He flushed the toilet. He looked in the mirror. His lip had whiskers growing. After he washed his face he scratched at the pimples on his nose and chin. He tasted the pus on his finger. The sound of the car cued up all this anxiety. He buried his face in the shower curtain. He turned away and killed the lights. He saw the stripe of light at the threshold. He stood in the kitchen after he walked into it. The rain was rhythm on the roof. Hague heaved. He spoke to Karen. She ate from this bag of chips. It was booze she smelled like. She said *Honey*. She said he needed to feed the dog. Karen asked him why he was at the back door. Hague told her that he just wanted to see them. She ruffled his hair, told him that he should take a shower. She told him that he should wash his hair. He mumbled as he walked outside. He called Henry's name. It was because he didn't see him. Karen walked out the door. It was because Hague was running in circles shouting the dog's name. When he found him he was on the side of the driveway, foam spewing from his mouth and nose. She said don't worry. She said it looks like he ate something. Hague filled a bucket with hose water. The dog didn't move. He sniffed at it. Karen looked down at Henry because she walked over to Hague. They stood in the rain. She cuffed the dog's snout and knocked his muzzle into the bucket. *Drink Henry.* He snorted. Hague stood there. He chased her into the house. He shouted at her. He screamed. *You drunk fucking bully.* It was what he screamed. She slammed the refrigerator door. She stared at him. He ran outside. The dog wasn't moving. He was laying in a rank and black pool. It poured from his mouth. It stuck in his fur. The kid fell down. He picked up the dog's head and poured water from the bucket down his throat. It just spilled out. The dog's eyes were dead spaces on his face. His stomach heaved and the kid was covered in the sick. Hague screamed and moaned. Nothing moved. He carried the dog's body inside. Karen asked him what the hell is going on. He put the dog on the rug. When she saw the crook of the dog's neck she knew. Hague paced all wide eyed. He grabbed this bottle off the table and threw it at her. He circled before he fell to his knees next to the dead dog. When he broke his hand it was because he pounded the floor with his fist and didn't stop. He lay down, rested his head on the dead sopping mess. He held his wrist. He yelled and sobbed and gagged. It split Karen's head. Hague spoke to Henry. He said *I wish I could be with you.* Karen smacked him. She told him not to talk like that.

WINTER

Hague stood there. He let himself fall forward. His face was pressed against the glass sliding door. His nose felt all closed and swollen. His eyes teared. Frozen condensation made his jaw ache. The white light coming through the window meant that something was infinite. He thought that, tried to. He just stood there. The world, the room, they spun into his vision. The week before Christmas Tuesday came home. She knocked on the door, she came into his room. He shrugged when she asked where Karen was. He said *She was here*. He said *It was yesterday or something*. Tuesday hugged him and she didn't let go. She said she was sorry about Henry. He buried his face into her shoulder. She asked him if he was eating. She said he felt skinny. On Christmas she told him it was ok that he didn't get her anything. He unwrapped the candy bars she brought him from school. He unwrapped the pack of bluebooks. *It's for you to draw in.* It was the morning and Karen slept through it. In the afternoon she said she was going out. She left then. Tuesday's breath steamed the window because she breathed on it. They drew on it with their fingers. She drew holly on his cast with scented markers. It was mint and cherry. They sat on the couch as he watched her play solitaire. He watched her until everything was just so still. She nudged him, she told him it was late, *Let's hit the hay, k?* He lay there in bed. The dark was so much he couldn't see but he just knew it. He shoved his face into his pillow. It was what vague shelter he could cobble. He had this dream that was so horrible. He jumped off a bridge so he would stop feeling so sad. When he stepped off that was it. The wind and rain disappeared. It was all black then. He couldn't know that but he knew he never could so he knew that it meant that he was awake. He gagged when he breathed. His lids peeled at his eyes. He had this daydream about his dream.

It was what lame crap he could assemble considering. He thought that if he killed himself then horrible would only be the last thing he felt before stuff disappeared. The lame thought's fucked appeal had this sheen. He couldn't muster a tarnish, try as he might. When he got out of bed Tuesday was asleep and the house was quiet. He walked through the yard. Dried leaves rushed against the chain link fence and he felt like he could see through it and himself and everything. There was a pool of oil where the car had been. There was a metal bowl filling with rain. Inside, he knocked on Tuesday's door but he was too soft and she was asleep. He just stood there. He walked into his room. When he sat on his bed he kicked the carpet until his toes bled through his socks. It was something he felt. He fell back. He construed to build a simple and idiotic machine… his belt, the ceiling fan. The story his thoughts scrawled was the dumbest fucking thing in the world: *When the chair tipped the world ended.* It was just a straight line and any idiot could draw it.

Tuesday cut Hague down then fell down. She laid him on the bed and threw open the drapes. She screamed his name but it was all quiet. The sunlight disappeared into the shadows covering Hague's bed. Tuesday held his head up, she tilted it back. She felt his glands under her thumb. She pressed her ear against his chest. She shook and begged him. She begged and begged. If there was a god what she said would be a prayer but there isn't so it couldn't be and they were fucked. Tuesday kissed his salty cheek and smelled his sour hair. She lay down next to him. The air moved against them. She could see the light coming through the window. She closed her eyes. It was so she would stop seeing it.

PART TWO:
FAKE JULY

The passages will never lead anywhere, the doors will always be shut.
– Jean Rhys

FALL

At the end of September Tuesday got an earache. It shot down her jaw. She was a shape on her bed beneath the drapes and the window behind them. When her palate swelled it pushed against her tongue. Chills wracked her shoulders as she stood in the shower. She held water in her mouth after she turned off the faucet. Her skin felt cold from the air. She just left her hair wet and put on her robe and brushed her teeth. The hall was empty. It smelled like perfume. In her room she thought that she should drink tea. It was because her roommate said to. She took the mug out of the microwave. It burned her hand. Her elbows and chest ached when she coughed. The room spun, her balance fell away. She looked at the building across from her dorm. Leaves swirled around the HVAC units on the roof. The light was there because she could see it on them. The bricks and windows didn't move until she fell back onto her bed. They cut to sky. When she squinted it cropped the sun. She reeled as she ran. It was down the hall and towards the bathroom. She threw up in the sink. The water flowed from the faucet. She just left it on. She sat on a toilet. The tile in the stall was damp. She slipped her foot from her flip flop and felt the cold on her heel and toes. Her face swelled with fluid. She rested it on her hands. Her sinuses ached beneath her fingertips when she pressed them. She stood in front of one of the mirrors. She dried her hand with a paper towel. A girl helped her back to her room. She rested her ear on a hot water bottle. Her cheek hardened and swelled beneath her skin. She massaged her neck. Her roommate touched her forehead. She told her that she needed to go to the doctor. Tuesday rubbed her finger against her thumb. Her roommate said she should call her mom. She said that she could wire Tuesday money. After Tuesday dialed the number Karen answered. The sound in the background was a buzzing wire. After she said *Hey Mom* it was the only thing that wasn't silent. Tuesday spoke and begged. She didn't say anything. She said *But I have this fucking fever.* She just lay there on the bed and stared into space. She put the phone down and shuddered. *What the fuck.* Her roommate said *Don't worry dear.* She told Tuesday that she could use her credit card. She said *No.* She told her that she wanted her to. Tuesday shivered as she walked down to the parking lot. Her roommate drove her across campus. The nurse swabbed the back of her throat. They gave her a shot of antibiotics. They gave her sulfa drugs. Her stomach burned when she took them. Her fever lasted a week. She lost weight because she lost her appetite. She mixed honey into vinegar and water. She gulped it. The skin on her chest and fingers swelled and peeled from her necklace and rings. Her roommate went home for the weekend and Tuesday forgot to eat. She only drank water. Her roommate didn't return. It was because she was in this accident. Her father picked up her stuff. He put it all in the back of a truck. Tuesday asked him if she was in the hospital. He only said she was ok. He kept saying it. Some girls started a collection for her. They had a bake sale. Her parents used the money to pay towards her funeral. *She'd taken a turn.* Tuesday's hand shook while she read that sentence in the email that her roommate's parents had sent out. She didn't feel it because her hands and everything were numb. She closed the email, her laptop. There's no way Tuesday could think about it. She didn't. They let Tuesday drop her classes, the college did. A friend of this guy she knew was looking for a housemate. She got a job and moved out of the dorms. She bought a mattress at The Salvation Army. She put it on the floor. Her room was tiny. It was a studio in the otherwise unfinished second floor. She couldn't open her dresser drawers all the way without standing on her mattress. There was this bigger bedroom for rent on the first floor but it cost more. Tuesday just lay in bed and drank echinacea tea. She ate rice and frozen pizza. Her mother didn't have her address because she didn't give it to her. She got a cell phone. When she held her hand up to a candle she didn't feel anything. It was because she was only thinking about touching it because she was in bed and the candle was on her dresser. Her water had been cold until the ice melted. The glass was empty. There was something at the bottom. The candle wick extinguished because the tea light had melted down. Then it turned dark, the room and everything.

Tuesday's housemate was named Ingrid. They stood in the kitchen together. Ingrid said she realized that she recognized her from this class they'd had. Tuesday was nibbling on a cracker. Ingrid said cheers as she clinked her beer bottle against her water glass. Tuesday didn't know what to say. She smiled, she looked down and away. Ingrid said she was drunk. She told her that she was going to bed. Tuesday shut off the light. The kitchen was dark then and she stood in it. When she walked into her room she got into bed. The rain started and it didn't let up. Damp drafts came through the walls and from around the windows. She pulled her blanket over her head. She had to buy a raincoat because the jacket she had soaked through to her skin. Ingrid invited her to her boyfriend's for Thanksgiving. They walked in the drizzle carrying platters of food in cardboard boxes. The wine they drank with dinner was sour. Tuesday drank coffee afterward. Her stomach settled then. The apartment was hot from the oven. Something warm spread across Tuesdays cheeks. Ingrid's boyfriend talked about leaving his Datsun at their house. It was because he was going to be going to Guatemala. Tuesday asked him if it ran. He started to talk. Ingrid laughed, she said *Honey,* kissed him. Tuesday looked down because she wanted to leave because she thought they wanted to be alone. She didn't get up. Ingrid put her hand on her shoulder. She poured her more coffee. That night she lay in bed and her eyes strained towards the ceiling. Her jaw and head cramped then. She fell asleep all headachy and sobbing.

WINTER

Ingrid had a going away party for her boyfriend after classes broke. Tuesday didn't know any of their friends. She drank wine. She walked around the room until she had drunken so much that she had to sit down. It was because all the light in the room had narrowed then spun. When she woke up she walked into the bathroom. She had diarrhea. She gagged when she brushed her teeth. A few days later the house was empty. Ingrid had gone home. Tuesday stayed. Ingrid had asked her if she was sure when she hugged her before she left. She asked her why she wasn't going home. Tuesday said it was because her mom was a selfish bitch. She said it was because she didn't want to see her. Ingrid looked into her eyes. When Tuesday was alone she turned on the furnace and all the lights. On Christmas she just slept because she didn't have to work. When she woke up it'd been a year since Hague died. She stood there and looked out the window. Everything was grey because the sky was white. Fog came in, it gave way to rain. It hit the peeling side of the garage in waves. She watched that happen. It was drapes that she closed. She felt cold regardless. It was because everything was. She boiled water for coffee, looked under the sink for paper towels. After she peed she blew her nose. She sat at the kitchen table with the lights off. She just stared into the distance like the wall she was facing was some great length away. A year ago she'd held Hague as this cut belt unwound then slackened. She thought that and repeated the thought. She kept until it was just these images that disappeared when she tried to focus on them. The wall hung still. Her welled eyes were behind it. Time that passed was changing light. These shadows reminded her of other shadows but Hague was standing in front of those so she blinked. She made it upstairs because that's where she aimed for. When she moved towards something she moved away from everything else. Tuesday just lay on her side and hugged her knees to her chest. She held them so tight she shook. She stopped. She just lay there and nothing stopped.

Ingrid came back after New Years. She rented the third room out. It was to a girl named Rachel. Ingrid's eyes were bright in the lamp light of the living room. Rachel and Tuesday were hanging out with her. She said that they should take the Datsun out for a ride. She said *Come on.*

Rachel and Ingrid walked into the kitchen. Tuesday stood outside. She opened the car door and pushed the passenger seat forward. She climbed into the back. Burns pocked the lamb's wool seat covers. The car started after

Ingrid played with the ignition. She drove them through the suburbs and out into the fields that surrounded the city. They took the freeway past malls and lights and stores. Ingrid blasted music. The door panels rattled because of the speakers. The exit they took was lit by a gas station sign. They drove on a road that was gravel and dark, thus empty. Rachel and Ingrid passed a can of beer back and forth. The road ran parallel to the freeway. Tuesday closed her eyes. She opened them. Flooded floodplains were glassy planes. They rode over railroad tracks. When Tuesday turned she looked. The freeway looked like lights tracing the shape of the freeway. Fence posts spun away against the darkness. Rachel and Ingrid spoke and smoked. Rachel cracked a tall boy. When she passed it back Tuesday said she didn't feel like drinking. Then she didn't say anything. She took it, sipped on the can until it was empty. The booze made the world stretch out until it just lasted forever. She tilted her head back. She looked out the back window. It was all a smudgy arena. That's what she saw. She watched the lights of the city as they approached it from a ways off. Her thoughts and the night just drowned in the shimmer. Their street was a hill and it didn't have any streetlights. The car began to rattle as Ingrid pulled it into the driveway. It was all shadows because it was between two houses. Tuesday coughed because of the cigarette smoke. She stepped in a puddle because it'd rained and the driveway was packed dirt and level. It was because she was too buzzed to pay attention. She said *Fuck*. She stumbled as she walked inside. The house was old. The foundation was bricks and cement. The floor shifted beneath their feet when they walked. Ingrid stood in her room with her. She said that the smell was coming from the carpet. She told her to nail a tarp down over it. Tuesday bought old blankets and laid them over that. Her room was on the side of the house. The stairs led right to it. Her window showed an alley. With the angle of the light her room was all golden in the afternoon. The days were so short. The tree limbs shifted in the wind. Rain washed away snow. It all turned to ice when the sky turned clear. It wore on. Tuesday walked home in the dry cold at night. She peeled off her scarf and hat. She left them where they were. She had to hang fly paper from a tack because flies filled her room. They poured through a crack in the ceiling that lead to the attic.

SPRING

Tuesday's room was humid because the window was painted closed. Rachel gave her a putty knife and a hammer. The sill was nicked and dented then. Paint chips flecked the panes like they'd been sprayed. She rubbed this candle stub on the window rails. The bank sent her her student loan instead of to the college. She cashed it then closed her account. She quit her job and didn't register for classes. In the shower she shaved her legs, under her arms. She pulled her wet hair back into a bun. Downstairs Ingrid had a friend over. Music and voices rose up the stairs and through the walls. Tuesday heard thunder as she walked downstairs. Ingrid said that she had something to tell them. She said that she got a job house sitting. It was an old farmhouse 90 miles out of town, she'd get paid even with the free rent. That's what she said. Ingrid asked Tuesday and Rachel to move with her. She said that she'd split the money. She said that they could just end the lease in town *Because, man, fuck the landlord.* Rachel laughed, she smiled. Ingrid invited her friend Beth. Beth said *Of course.* Tuesday waived her hand. She spoke and stopped. She sopped what had spilled with a napkin. The table veneer looked darker when she looked at it. She had been saying something. Beth looked askance. Her pink gums gave way to white teeth. Outside the window the rain on the patio made steam come off of it. Tuesday sat on her hands. She swallowed water from a glass. She said *Of course.* A week later they fit all of their stuff into one moving truck. Sunlight showed on the freeway because it was all flat out to the house. The property was huge. They swept the floors and scrubbed the kitchen cupboards before they moved in. They furled the sheets that had covered the furniture. Tuesday carried her stuff to her room. Dead insects were dried inside the light fixtures. She cleaned the windows with vinegar and newsprint. The ground floor smelled like soap, then incense. The air cooled and the wind picked up. They walked out to the back porch to watch the sun set. Tuesday put her hands on her hips. She squinted, stopped. The yard was flat until the fences that surrounded the fields that surrounded the house. Shadows came in over all of it. It was night everywhere then. Tuesday thought that. She didn't turn on the light in her room because it was true that it was dark. That's what she thought.

SUMMER

Beth made wine from raspberries and Oregon-grape. She made jam from rose petals and peppercorns. Ingrid brewed beer. She used chamomile instead of hops. They stored the bottles under the house to keep them cool. Rachel edged around the hedges. She put mason jars filled with lilacs all over the house. When it rained they all stayed inside. Rachel said her room sucked. She said it was the sound. She started to play her guitar in the living room because it didn't bother anyone. She said it was all the windows. Beth began to play with her. She bought a banjo at a thrift store. Ingrid had this old keyboard. Tuesday listened to them playing. She lay down on the couch.

She heard them as she fell asleep. When she woke up the room was empty. The windows showed light. It showed on her face. She just sat there. She lay in a warm bath to loosen her crooked neck. The girls ate dinner alfresco because of the heat. Ingrid spooned lentils with cilantro, corn dressed with lime. Tuesday watched brown ants devour aphids and spider eggs on an azalea. She washed her hands beneath an outdoor spigot. Someone'd left the door to the kitchen propped open with a brick. When they came inside the house was full of millers and nits. Tuesday swept the corner of the ceiling of her room with a broom. She sprinkled lavender oil onto light bulbs.

It was a month that the girls played together every day. Tuesday said they sounded so good. She said they should put on a show. The girls invited all their friends in town. They made this banner. It was to hang for when they played. They sewed together white bed sheets with red yarn and fat needles. Rachel came up with a name,

Shiva The Destroyer. When she drew it the letters looked more torn than scrawled. The girls decorated the banner with stencils. The beet juice they used looked like pooling rust not dripping blood. Tuesday cut shapes from sheets of colored felt. She arranged them, picked them up. She squirted glue, looked, waited. She chucked it all. Ingrid hugged her. She said it was ok. Tuesday said that she didn't know why she was crying. Beth's fingers blistered from playing so much. She held out her hands, guffawed. Rachel asked Tuesday if she could play drums. She told Tuesday that they could figure it out. The night of the show Rachel didn't want to start playing until the sun had set so they waited. Tuesday stood in the yard. Their friends' cars had turfed the lawn. The sky was clouds and light, all yellow and orange. It was black after that. Tuesday slapped at mosquitoes on her neck and arms. Inside she sat in half lotus with a coffee can, tambourines, and a cardboard box. She hit them with a drumstick and a mallet. Unzipped and splayed sleeping bags covered the living room floor. The music and Rachel's voice and the backdrop were lit by sandalwood candles. The windows were open because of the heat. Ingrid had filled a canning pot with lemonade and Beth's wine. The beer had spoiled because she hadn't used hops. Rachel lit a joint. She placed it in an ashtray. Her hands and vision steadied when she'd had something to drink, something to smoke. The music hummed and gained when it reflected off the ceiling. Rachel's lyrics were doom laden and inconsequential. Pussy willow branches tied with twine hid the torchieres. Tuesday's wrists clicked and swelled. Her ears rang when they stopped playing. She got a chill from the air moving and her sweat. She knew this guy Jorma who'd driven some friends up. She felt nauseous from the wine and lemonade. She poured herself some cognac in the kitchen, gulped it. She poured more, handed it to him. They walked out to his wagon. They folded the seats down and left the windows open while they lay there and shared the drink. When she woke up cold, she shrunk into his warm chest and arms. They'd used his jacket as a blanket. In the morning they all drove to the mountains to this lake. The beach they camped on was just the shore that the trees surrounded. They had their cars and tents. Ingrid and her boyfriend built a lean-to from wood they gathered. Dusk was the light dimming and the air turning cool. Tuesday sat on a log with Jorma.

The wind picked up and it began to rain. The surface of the water was what the wind looked like when it hit it. They built a fire ringed by rocks in the pine needles and brush on the edge of the trees. Tuesday had all this energy. It lit through her thoughts. She climbed this tree, hung from a branch, let go. It cracked and fell. She laughed and stood there. Rachel kicked it into the fire. Pinprick sparks floated through the pitch. When Tuesday fell down and rolled onto her back her head was resting on Jorma's lap. He leaned forward. He started to kiss her. The longer it was dark the colder it got. They had cases of beer that someone brought. Everyone sat around the fire. They drained bottles and cans down their throats. They ransacked their backpacks for condoms. The next morning Tuesday got out of the car. She peed in these trees. Rachel squatted in front of the fire. It was ashes. When she threw some balled newspaper on it flared. Ingrid boiled ground coffee in a sauce pan. She spooned the liquid so as to cool it. Tuesday held her hand over her cup to keep the rain out. They hiked around the lake. The trees broke and so did the kids. Tuesday looked at the water like there was something there but there wasn't so she turned away. She caught up with Jorma because he had waited for her. On the ride back to the house Jorma put his arm around her. She hugged him after he dropped her off. He held her when she did. The housemates took turns taking showers. It was the hot water heater. Tuesday just slept.

FALL

When the wind stopped and the furnace shut off the house was quiet. Beth moved back to town because of her boyfriend. Rachel planned another show. She said it would be a moving out party. Tuesday emailed Jorma. She told him to make sure that he made it. He wrote her back. *Totally.* The night of the show Tuesday got drunk with Rachel. Rachel started to panic about the show. It wracked her as she wrung her hands. They drank beer then gin. When Rachel knocked her glass over it broke and she shared Tuesday's. They kept sharing it. They stumbled out of Rachel's bedroom with their arms around each other. Tuesday concentrated on each step that she took.

Downstairs she stood at the landing. She saw Jorma, it was because he'd just gotten there. He'd brought this girl with him and Tuesday thought that they were together. Tuesday didn't look at him. When he tried to kiss her she walked away, slammed her door. The hall was silent when he stood there but inside her room sounded like her crying, slamming drawers. When she opened the door Jorma was gone. Everyone breathing in the living room steamed the windows. It condensed and ran and froze to the sills. The light from the moon and planets looked like they meant it to look that way. Ingrid poured coffee and brandy into a samovar. Tuesday made it downstairs. The girls wore leg warmers on their arms and beneath their skirts and petit coats. Tuesday knelt in front of her drums on the floor. She hit a tambourine with a timpani mallet. It just lay there. Rachel had this look on her face like each word meant so much. She mumbled, her playing stumbled. It was all lost in the echo and the din. The shaft of Tuesday's mallet hit the rim of a tabla and it felt different thereafter. She kept playing though. Because music is invisible she stared down through the whole set. Post gig, the girls huddled around the kitchen table and drank beer. Tuesday made this face. It looked to Ingrid like she did. When Ingrid hugged her Ingrid's boyfriend hugged her from behind. Ingrid said *Stupid boys.* Tuesday was standing because they were holding her up between themselves. In bed her head spun as she fell asleep. She woke and bathed. The water cooled and she kept laying in it. When she got out she vomited. She knelt naked before the toilet on a towel that was lying on the tile.

The girls all moved back to town. It was because the owners were coming back Ingrid moved in with her boyfriend. Rachel and Tuesday moved in together. They left boxes piled up all over the apartment. Shiva The Destroyer practiced at each other's places. Because of the neighbors they couldn't play as loud as Rachel wanted to. She recorded all their practices, edited them on her computer. It got harder for her to get a hold of Ingrid. Rachel said that Ingrid would rather fuck her boyfriend than play in a band. She started playing by herself. Tuesday was fine with it. She got a job working at this shop. She thought it was ok, that it was whatever. Rachel sold some books and some paintings she had for cash. It got warm. For a week the wind stopped coming in from the water. Rachel ran out of money and she got this part time job. She started dating this guy. When they broke up she sat on the couch and cried. Tuesday spent her lunches sitting on a bench in this park. She wore a sweater beneath her parka. She sat there so she could get off her feet. They hurt because of her shoes. After lunch one afternoon she took $20 from the register just because. At home she took off her skirt, put on a dress. Rachel said they got this letter. She said they were being evicted because of how loud her music was. Tuesday said *Fuck*. She told Rachel that her friend was having this party. Rachel said just to go, she said she didn't feel like going out. Tuesday frowned. She hugged her. Tuesday spent the twenty on a bottle of champagne. She walked down side streets until she got to her friend's house. White wash wore from the railing when she walked up the stairs. Her reflection in the window looked like she was wearing makeup because she was. She needed help with the champagne bottle. She found a knife to peel at the foil. Tuesday poured some for this girl because she asked her to. The champagne foamed and spilled when Tuesday poured herself more. The girl said something. Tuesday couldn't hear her above the music. The girl held out her glass. She smiled. Tuesday got dizzy, held the bottle with both hands by the neck. She still sipped from the bottle once it was warm. Her friend's house got packed. They ate hors d'oeuvres. There was a bubble bath in the bathroom. Tuesday sat down on this window seat. She looked and listened. Everything just happened. Her mouth was thick from something at the bottom of the bottle. A girl pushed a guy into the bathtub. People took pictures with their phones. Tuesday took off. She walked home with the champagne bottle in her hand. It was cold out but she wasn't. When she got home she and Rachel blasted music and danced. Tuesday took off her shoes. She squinted as she moved. She tripped then sat on the couch. After Rachel sat down next to her they just sat there. Rachel told Tuesday she thought she was so pretty. Tuesday was drunk and horny. She said *Rachel*. She kissed her. She tore off her jeans and her camisole.

Tuesday and Rachel rented a house on a side street. The driveway ran off an alley. They hung prayer flags from the awning. Rachel scrubbed at the patterns on the wallpaper. She repaired the peeled corners with paste. Tuesday stood on a ladder outside. When she poured water from a bucket she watched it run down the gutter. The breeze blew her hair into her face, it blew the rain against the windows. Rachel set up the second bedroom as their office. She told Tuesday that she wanted it for playing music. She unpacked boxes of their stuff. The desk was a card table. It was covered with jewel cases and cords. The dust in the air made her sneeze. She opened the door for air because she hadn't opened the window. Tuesday walked through the living room. Damp paintbrushes lay in the bathtub. The fan rattled against the air. Tuesday peed. She walked from the bathroom into the kitchen, from the kitchen into the living room. Their front steps led to a stoop. Green carpet wore down to gray cement. She sat down and tied her shoes. She zipped up her jacket.

The yard, it was what was inside the fence. Tuesday turned towards the house. The reflection on the garage window glared when she saw it. Twine tied around a tree trunk wore away when she picked at it with her thumbnail. Her foot slipped on a patch of mud when the grass gave way. Her jaw and forehead ached from the air. It was bright but it didn't heat a thing, the sun. Tuesday's shoes were soaked through the canvas. It was the rain. Her ankle was sore. It spread into her calf. Inside, she heard water running in the kitchen. She sat on the couch. She undid the knots in her laces. Her feet were numb against the floor. She held her hands beneath the faucet in the bathroom. When she said Rachel's name she was looking down and into the sink. Mud spun down the drain and she watched it spin until it disappeared.

Rachel said *You should*. She said *I want you to, I mean, she's your mother*. When she put her arm around Tuesday Tuesday lay there. The girls heard wind out the windows and rain on the roof. The sound died, rose and died. When Tuesday sat on the bed she had her feet on the carpet. She held her phone up to her ear. She turned up the volume because of the storm. The voice on the machine was a machine. It was the number they'd always had so she had to assume. When she spoke she said *Hey mom, it's twos.* She said *I just*, she inhaled, she said *I just wanted to know how you're doing?* After she said *Here's my number* she said it. Rachel sat down next to her. The glass that she handed her was full of wine. She asked her if she was ok. Tuesday set the glass down. Rachel's arms were bands that bound her. Rachel walked into the living room. When Tuesday got up she picked through the jewelry box on the dresser. She found an old pack of cigarettes. The filter fell off one when she broke it off. She walked into the kitchen. She lit the cigarette off a stove burner. After she walked into the living room she handed it to Rachel. She dragged, handed it back. They hadn't eaten, Rachel was gaspy and buzzed. Tuesday opened the door because they were dizzy. She stubbed the cig on the stoop. She flicked the butt. Inside, her voice cracked. She spoke about Hague and their father because Rachel asked her about them. Rachel's eyes and face were lit and glowing. Tuesday's thoughts then words were facts she summoned. After she got up she came back. Hague was the baby being bathed in the bathroom sink in the photo that she showed her. Her dad was the hand holding his head above the water. The shadow in the mirror above the sink looked like her father's face when she looked at it and thought about what his face looked like. Her thoughts were images strung from moods. The vase on the table was the color of dirt if dirt was black. It was what she was looking at while she talked about him. She said that he smelled like cologne, that he felt like terrycloth. She talked about when Hague was older. She said that the summer when he turned 7 he was obsessed with dressing like him. Tuesday told her that it bled into fall. That Halloween he wore dad's clothes. He had shirt sleeves running down to his feet, his feet were at the knees of his jeans. He looked so goofy when he smiled. I stole the chocolate from his sack. Nine months later dad had killed himself. The room was quiet and Rachel looked at her. Tuesday would just fall down and keep falling if she could. It was that she was drunk. It was everything. She got up to blow her nose. She picked up her phone. When she pressed buttons the screen changed. Then she hung up. It was before it just rang unanswered for the second time. Rachel lay down. Her back arched and her sweater hitched. She looked up then fell asleep. Tuesday finished her glass and then her own. She leaned forward and held her face in her palms, she picked it up. When she walked into the office she stepped over the crap piled all over. The box she was looking for was dented and taped. She lay down in bed with it. The cracked lid proffered vegetal smells. Her thoughts swam, blended. She woke exhausted. Rachel was at work. When Tuesday picked up her phone she dialed a number. She told someone she was sick. She sat down with the box and stole her shaking hands against a draft. It was full of photographs. Hague was in each of them because the box only had photographs of him in it. The light from the window dimmed. Her throat ached and her eyes bulged as the pale light flensed all these details from the photographs. Her mouth formed these shapes. The photo she was holding was something from school. His parted hair peeled back on his skinny neck. The light in his eyes was just the lighting but they'd be lit forever if she never looked away. She thought that.

Tuesday got fired from her job because she quit showing up. Rachel got more hours. They made her full time. All the money she made went to rent. Her bike was stolen and their neighbor gave them a car. Rachel spent her savings to get it running. They lay in the dark together. She told Tuesday that she didn't need to do anything that she didn't want to. She told her that she would take care of her. Tuesday curled her face into the crook of Rachel's neck. Her job sent her last check. After she cashed it she used a rubber band, put it in her dresser drawer. If the mirror was a mirror then the world didn't exist. She just stood there. Her eyes were closed because she closed them after she lay down. When she woke up she heard the fan. She opened her eyes. She was sharing a pillow with Rachel. She got up, made her coffee. She thought she should request her transcripts. She thought she should look into finishing her degree. When she thought about what money she'd need, she thought that money equaled impossible and impossible equaled impossible to think about. She called about applying for unemployment. She sat on the couch and drank coffee. She ate lunch because she thought that she should eat something. When birds flew into the window it was a thuddy chime. Cats stormed the hedges. She pounded on the window. She chased them off. The screen door slammed behind her. When a cat dropped a bird at her feet its eyes just looked and kept looking. Tuesday didn't until she did. Things fell inward. She pressed her hands over her mouth. Rachel stood in the kitchen and stirred a pot. She said something. She poured some soymilk from a carton. Tuesday stood in the threshold between the living room and the kitchen. It was all light. That's what it looked like. They ate dinner on the couch. They watched a movie on Rachel's laptop because of the DVD player. They were drinking cheap wine. It made her dizzy and gave her a headache. She fell asleep. When she woke up in the dark she was kissing Rachel, pulling off her pajamas.

WINTER

The rain turned to snow. It built up on the roads. When Rachel got home on Christmas eve she had take out and groceries. They spent Christmas eating. Tuesday set out glasses and napkins. They watched movies on network television. Tuesday sobbed for an hour as she lay in bed without Rachel knowing because she had told her she needed to lie down because she was hungover and her stomach hurt. It was because two years ago Hague had died. It was because when she had tried to call her mother she'd gotten the same voicemail she'd gotten months previous. Her salty tears stung where her nails pressed her cheeks. She rubbed cold cream into her skin. The glare coming through the windows came through the room and off of every surface. They drew the curtains tight. They walked to the corner store once it was dark. The parking lot was empty. It was closed. When they walked back to the house Tuesday said *Curse the cold*. Her thrust fists pounded the bottoms of her pockets. When they got back home she realized she didn't have her keys. Rachel said *Are you fucking serious?* They pried at the storm windows with their numb fingers. They called the landlord. Inside Tuesday held her hands beneath the faucet in the bathroom. Rachel closed the door to their office. She said she had something to record. To Tuesday it sounded like a guitar being played behind a closed door because that's what it was. Tuesday sipped on red wine. It was to feel warmer. 30 minutes later she was all flush, sad and lit. It was because she drank until her glass, then the bottle was empty. It was because of how it tasted and how she wanted to keep tasting it. She got up. Rachel didn't see anything when she walked into the room. Tuesday came at her all red faced and crying. When she tried to hug her she tripped. It was because her tears razed the world until it was just a gray wash. She knocked shit all over the fucking place when she stumbled. The laptop fell from the amp Rachel'd balanced it on. Cables tore from their inputs. She said *Rachel hold me, I want you to hold me*. When Rachel thought *Just get the fuck out of here Tuesday*, Tuesday sobbed. She stormed for the hall, slammed the door. It was because Rachel had screamed it.

SPRING

Rachel had to travel for work. Tuesday told her she could leave the car at the airport. She said she wouldn't need it. Rachel looked at her. She said all I need is you. She asked her what was wrong. Tuesday shrugged, she looked at the curb. She kicked at it. Rachel just held her until a chill flushed her skin. After the car was packed they stood outside. The sun was low. It was cold and bright. Tuesday wrapped her arms around her waist. Rachel told her that it would be ok. She said *It will only be a couple days*. She said she loved her. After she hugged her Tuesday was emptied of everything except anxiety. If every car and plane stopped moving and never moved again, if Rachel never left her, she had never wished for anything so much in her life. Rachel drove away and she just wasn't there until Tuesday went inside. Then no one was. Tuesday didn't eat. She fell asleep. When she woke up it was because her phone was ringing. The calls were from a blocked number. Tuesday didn't answer them. When she called her voicemail it was her mother's voice that she heard. Her slurred speech was graffiti on the bright smear behind it. Tuesday hung up. She re-listened to the message. Her mom didn't give her a number. After she hung up she called their old home number. The message told her that she dialed it wrong, it told her that it was disconnected. Tuesday stared into space. She looked into her reflection in the window next to the bed. It was dark because it was night, still. She checked and rechecked their old home number. She just kept checking it. She got up after she lay there. The refrigerator light's glare was warm because it was something. Tuesday stood there and stared into it. She drank a bottle of beer to get tired. It didn't work, she stayed awake. She just drank more then. She was drunk at dawn. It'd just been dark, what she'd sat in up until then. She was thinking about what she would say to Karen should she speak to her. She said something out loud and then her kaput brain lost it. She gulped from the bottle she was holding, felt her hair. She gasped and gagged. It was because of how as the sun rose she thought it looked like it could never fall. It was because all this stuff rushed at her. She picked up a beer. She pried the crown cap with a disposable lighter. It foamed over when she back washed into it. It covered her face and blouse. She splashed water with her cupped palms. Steam rose from the sink beneath the running faucet. She dried her hands on her jeans. The white grout was brown. Her face felt dry from the hand soap. She passed out on the couch. When she woke up she looked at her watch like it mattered. She poured hot water from a kettle onto a teabag in a mug. After she waited she removed it. She stirred in marmalade with a spoon. Her tea got cold because she didn't drink it. The windows just looked like grey rain because when the clouds came in there was no sun. The storm got louder. She knelt on the couch and looked out over the back of it. She saw no end and no way out. She listed to the left because she was dizzy. The bottle she grabbed had something left at the bottom. She knew the window was cold because she felt it. She just saw the houses around theirs. Below the clouds the horizon was a light coming from where no light could exist. Tuesday stumbled as she walked. She stood outside the front door. She closed her eyes and breathed. She was beneath the awning, beneath a leaking gutter seam. Something crawled through her hair. She felt it. Something dark washed over a mind that looked like the sky at night after you erased the stars and everything.

Rachel got home the next night. Tuesday heard her key in the deadbolt. Rachel told Tuesday she was exhausted. Tuesday poured her wine and ordered pizza. She hugged her until Rachel set down her glass. She didn't let go. Rachel said she felt gross from all the planes and hotels. She said she needed to take a shower. When she got out she lay down. She fell asleep. Tuesday stood beside the couch and watched her. She peeled the cheese from a piece of pizza. The next morning Tuesday felt humidity and heat on her face. Rachel hugged her. She used her hands to brush her bangs out of her eyes. Rachel said *Twos*. Tuesday's eyes narrowed and her jaw tightened. She said *It's just so fucking hot*. Rachel smiled. The air was still. Tuesday got heat rashes from wearing her bra. She said *Let's go out*. She said *Let's see a movie*. Rachel said she needed to chill. Tuesday paced. They ran fans to deal with the heat and that's what the house sounded like. Tuesday broke out across her cheeks. When she turned her head her reflection changed in the mirror. She felt more pimples beneath her skin. She stood in front of the fridge and opened bottles of beer. She drank them till there was none left. She thought it was to calm herself down. Rachel sat cross legged in front of the TV. She held a GameCube controller. The window behind her was a glary sheet. Tuesday's nausea was a pulsing swell. She rested both arms on the sink edge when she leaned forward. She walked into the living room. She kicked over the coffee table. A candle dented the wall. It was strewn shards on the floor. It was because Rachel didn't pause her game. Tuesday knew that. She started crying. She said she would clean it up. She said she was sorry. Once she was kneeling she couldn't move. She screamed. She said *You left me*, she said *You can't leave me.* Tuesday reached her hands behind her head. Her fingers twined together. She leaned forward and down. When she stared at Rachel, her face was red and sopping. She stormed out the screen door and Rachel chased after her in bare feet. Rachel stopped. She turned back. Tuesday fell down at a bus stop and inhaled through her nose. Tears and snot ran down her face. She moved behind the shelter. No one saw her. She touched her hands to her thighs. She palmed her kneecaps. The sun moved. The sky was blue. A hummingbird was a dragonfly. The moon was the color of the clouds. She walked home. Rachel sobbed on the couch. Her foot was bleeding. Her footprints were a trail of tacky splotches. She slammed the bathroom door. When it opened it was after Tuesday had borne her weight against it. It was after she had kicked at the locked handle. Rachel pulled away. She said *Tuesday, what the fuck?* She said *You're scaring me.* Tuesday tried to hug her and when Rachel pushed her she fell backwards into the tub. She reached her hand down as she fell. A bottle of shampoo dropped. Rachel slapped her. Tuesday stared forward. She saw where the lock bolt had shredded the doorframe beneath the strike plate. She threw up into the tub drain. Rachel didn't see it because she was gone then. Tuesday stared up and forward.

Tuesday drank iced tea with lemon. She sat on the toilet while Rachel took a shower. The bathroom smelled like mildew and moist air. It smelled like conditioner. She drew lips on the mirror with lipstick. She handed Rachel a towel. Rachel wrapped herself in it. Tuesday spread lotion on her arms and elbows. They got into bed. Rachel lay flat. She turned, looked at Tuesday. Rachel kissed her. Her damp hair hung down. She said *Happy birthday*. The package she handed her was wrapped in tissue paper. It was tied with yarn. It was a framed photograph of them. Rachel said *I love you so much*. Tuesday picked up her phone because it was ringing. She said *Oh my god, mom*. It was quiet after that. It was because the sentence her mother spoke ran. After Karen stopped talking she said *Thank you*. Tuesday said she was living on the peninsula. Karen said she had some cash. She said that she could rent a car and drive down to see her. Tuesday asked her what happened to the car. She said to never mind. She said she'd drive to see her herself. Karen began to name dates. She talked so fast. Tuesday repeated something. She hung up. She was shaking. Rachel said *What the fuck?* Tuesday said *It was my mother.*

SUMMER

After Tuesday peed in the grocery store bathroom, she walked back to the car. She chewed her nails. Her torn cuticle just hung off. Blood specked tissue was wrapped around her thumb. The car smelled like the hand soap from the bathroom. It was just heat when she exhaled. The radio had a clock on it. She gritted her teeth while she squinted her eyes. She ran against the traffic when she crossed the street. The main drag hit a side street. Tuesday turned down it and another. Her mother was at a cement picnic table. Everything was shaded by trees and paved by cobblestones. She said hello. She didn't hug her because she didn't stand up. She asked her if she ate pizza. Tuesday took a slice out of the box that was sitting between them and held it with a napkin. She looked Karen in the eye. She smiled and so did Karen and everything was quiet. She reached out and held her hand. Karen told her she had something for her. A little something for your birthday. Her breath smelled like the gum she was chewing and the cigarette she was smoking. The borders banking her syllables were washed by whatever she'd been drinking. She reached for the box under her purse. She said *Open it*. She said *Tuesday, open it*. Tuesday's fingernails peeled at the seams of the paper. They peeled at the corners of the tape. Karen said *Tuesday, why'd you break off contact with me?* Tuesday looked at the earrings in the jewelry box. She said *I just…* She paused because she was swallowing. Karen said that she didn't understand. Everything was quiet. She said *Tuesday I need you*, she said *Tuesday why'd you leave me all alone? We're all we have after what happened to poor Haguey.* Tuesday sat there. She told her that what happened to Hague was that he killed himself. She said *What happened was that I found him, and it was a day before you found out because you were off drunk god knows where.* Karen asked her why she was angry at her.

Tuesday said *Why didn't you return my call for so long mom?*
This sycamore tree spread out above them and they were
in all this shade. Tuesday felt her cheeks with her hand.
She felt this flush. She started to cry when she said *Why
couldn't you be sober to meet me?* Karen's voice slurred while
Tuesday stared into her unfocused eyes. She said *Tuesday,
frankly I don't even know why you bothered to call me.* Tuesday asked her why they couldn't meet at home. She asked
her what the fuck did you do with the car? Karen said
something. She asked Tuesday what the fuck she knew.
Tuesday picked up the box and threw it at her. Karen just
sat there. The park was a dead end off a side street. Stairs
cut right up a hill. It wasn't empty but it didn't matter.
Tuesday's back was to everything. When Karen shouted
Twos, I love you Tuesday kept walking. Her hand shook
and the key missed the car door until she used both hands.
She drove all the way instead of taking the ferry. When she
made it into the front door it was dark. Her legs and wrists
were numb. She cried and Rachel held her. She opened a
beer. She drank one, another. She closed the bathroom
door and sat on the toilet. She closed her eyes. When she
woke it was from the cold that come from the air and ev-

ery surface. She was nauseous because she was dizzy. She picked up her phone to call her mom. After she threw it she punched the wall. Rachel stood in the doorway then. Tuesday was curled on the bathmat. She got up. Tuesday said *She's my mother*. Rachel said *She's a worthless bitch because she makes you feel this way.* Tuesday nodded. Tuesday had this bad taste from the IPA. She cupped her hands beneath the faucet and gasped at the pouring water. She choked as she gulped.

Fall

The train tracks cut beneath the freeway. Outside the city was the horizon Tuesday saw when she stared down the rails like they were a line that connected to someplace. The tracks ran through a gully then the edge of a forest. Tuesday walked in the shade such as it was. She balanced on rimed and slick rails with her arms stretched out. The world was full of light that showed everything. The water was just water and islands and boats abutting the bluff below her. She hucked the stubby she'd been sipping from because it was empty. She stumbled back. It was her buzz. She didn't fall. She walked with her head down then. She found their house because she knew where it was. Rachel strummed her unplugged guitar. Tuesday just sat on the couch. Rachel looked down at the one mic pointed at the body of her guitar and the other pointed at the neck. Cables ran into the bathroom. They ran beneath her feet. An amp was sitting in the bathtub. The microphone that was pointed at it was plugged into her four-track. She played her 4 track into her laptop. She burned CD's and sent them out. She got a letter from a label. They wanted to release her demos as is. They sent her a contract. Rachel cried. Tuesday jumped up and down. She screamed that she was so proud. The girls went out to dinner. They spent more money than they had. They had cocktails, then wine, then cocktails. When they woke up the next day it was afternoon. The front window was rain, it gave way to sun. Orange light reflected off of standing water. Rachel's friend called them in the evening. She invited them to a party. They got dressed up. Tuesday told Rachel that she was better with makeup than she was. The girl's friend had pushed all her furniture against the walls. People ate in the kitchen. Somebody started to play records. Tuesday switched from vodka and soda to beer. Rachel was talking and laughing in the middle of the room. Tuesday walked up to her. Rachel was glowing and slurred. She kissed Tuesday's forehead. She cupped her bent neck then walked away. This girl told her somebody was doing something to their car. Rachel had the keys in her purse. Tuesday scanned the room for her. She didn't see her. She found her purse and grabbed the keys. Their car was blocking the neighbor in. Tuesday said *I'm so sorry, oh my god*. She said it to this guy. He told her to just move her fucking car. Her hand was shaking as she tried to fit the key into the door. She parked the car around the block. She walked inside and grabbed a beer. She talked to this guy. The neighbor was such a dick. That's what she told him. She went looking for Rachel. Carpeted stairs sounded hollow beneath her feet. The second floor was all open. She walked across it to the back porch. Rachel was on the porch on the second floor. She was sitting on this guy's lap. His arm was around her waist. She was kissing him. Tuesday turned around and left. She pushed through people and ran around the corner. She sat in the car. She drove it home. She grabbed what cash she had and filled her backpack with stuff. It was dark and she was drunk. She stopped at a gas station and bought coffee. She filled the car up then got on the on-ramp and drove.

The snow began to stick when Tuesday hit the pass. She felt it in the handling. It was dawn and her hands were shaking when she came on these trucks pulled off onto the shoulder. Someone had lit flares. She saw 2 truckers leaning against a wheel well with their hoods pulled on. They just looked at her. When she took the switchback the car slid and drifted sideways. She kept driving. There was this tunnel for the road and the tire tracks before her headed into it. What she saw where the headlight showed was flat and black. It was because her eyes were fucked. It was because she hadn't stopped since she left. When she let off the gas she coasted. When the foothills gave way it was coastal plains they gave way to. She made out signs above the fences. She made out clouds above the trees. When she pulled off it was to pee. She cried because it felt so good to close her eyes then. She couldn't stop so she didn't. The girl at the counter looked at her when she returned the key. The gas station was just something she left. The road was a floating bridge. It traced the shape cut into the rocks that broke at the madronas above her. Railings became curbs. She coasted through an intersection in this town. It was because she couldn't make out the red light. It was because she couldn't make out anything. She pulled into a space with a meter. She just sat there. With her eyes such as they were the world was just sheets of color. She blinked then held them closed. She opened them. Tuesday felt punched, crushed. It was the spreading dim coming from the sun through the clouds. It was because it made the world look gutted. It was because it made the world look like something that'd been shot.

Tuesday parked the car a block from a marina. She could see it across this empty lot. A storm came in from the water. It was the wind that carried it. Tuesday shut off the wipers and watched the hood. The rain pooled and ran. She locked the door after she got out. She checked it. It was a puddle that she stepped in when she fell off the curb. It was how her foot had slipped and her ankle had twisted. She bought a coffee at this shop. It hurt when she swallowed. She ran the car to warm it up. She had her socks on the dash vents. It chapped her lips and made her eyes itch. She used her jacket sleeve to wipe off the window. She checked her socks. Her cash was spread on the passenger seat because she was counting it. She killed the engine, looked at her phone. It didn't show any calls because nobody had called her. The screen said the battery was dying. She called Rachel. She started speaking because it was Rachel's voicemail that answered. Her voice was filtered through her sobbing. She said *I don't hate you.* She kept repeating it. She stopped. When she started speaking again she said *It's myself that I hate.* She paused and exhaled. Her voice wavered and whispered. She said *I fucking hate you for making me hate myself.* She talked to herself after she hung up. She said *I need to sleep.* The thought ran over and over in her head and she kept saying it. The rain was so loud. It drowned out all other sounds. She knew her lips were moving. She knew she was speaking because she could feel her lips and her jaw.

Her ears rang after it all stopped. She drove around until she passed this motel on a dead end. After it there was just a marine mechanic, a cold storage warehouse. She doubled back. The parking lot was empty and the street lamps that lit it were still on. She drove through ruts and potholes filled with water. The office was a TV sans sound. It was coffee burning and broken window shades. Of the hundred bucks she had, the room would cost $45. She said *I only have $35*. The guy shook his head, she dug her hand in her pocket, she grabbed a 10. The security bars on the window were rusted hurricane fencing. The room smelled like mildew and aldehydes. She turned on the baseboard heater. It smelled like burning dust. The wall behind the bed and the ceiling were stained brown with water damage. She brushed her teeth and washed her face. She tore a square of toilet paper and blew her nose. She lay down in the bed wearing her clothes beneath the sheets. She was starving and it was the starving that made her so weak that she just lay there. It was the starving that was so strong it woke her up. The clock said it was 20 minutes later than it had been. There was a coffee maker and stuff in her room but no coffee. She filled one of the plastic cups with water and stirred in sugar and creamer. She gulped it. She hurled and spit saliva into the sink. She held back her hair and pushed back her bangs. Her hand shook when she picked up her wadded cash. She walked the blocks of the drag. The only place that was open was Chinese. Fluorescent light lit off the Formica booth. The tofu and vegetables in brown sauce came with white rice and free tea. She ate off the styrofoam plate with a plastic fork. Her phone meant nothing without the charger, it meant nothing without Rachel calling it. The pawn shop was on the access road next to the freeway. The 15 dollars they gave her was 5 gallons of gas. It was 125 miles of driving. It took her a second to figure it out. The man behind the counter grinned when he handed her the cash. She wiped her nose on her sleeve. He told her to make sure she had herself a good day. She made it back to the motel. She collapsed on the bed while still holding her key. She started crying. It was the not sleeping. It was because it all overwhelmed her. She couldn't stand the room because it stank and everything felt gross. She wanted Rachel holding her in the cold bed because then it wouldn't be. When she thought that everything else disappeared. If she hadn't already written off the possibility of ever speaking to her again then she'd just get in the car and drive home, but she had, so she didn't. That's why she screamed her name. She buried her face in the pillow when someone pounded on the wall. She just lay there. It was all black, the white pillowcase she was staring into. She felt like she was blind, drowning. It was the world that was washing over her. When she thought she just thought she was fucked. Her sobbing gave her a headache. The light coming from beneath the hem of the drapes meant it was light out. She cried herself to sleep.

It was late in the morning when she woke up and it was the pounding on the door that did it. She did the chain on the latch. She told the guy from the desk to give her a fucking minute. She closed the door. When she walked out of the bathroom she washed her hands. The walls made this sound. It was the water in the pipes. That got quiet. The pounding started again. It was just what she heard. When she turned her back to the sink the room was there. She grabbed her backpack. She grabbed her keys off the bed. Her shoulders hunched from the weight. They were hunched from the cold. She opened the door. She looked down at her shoes. She didn't see that the guy wasn't there. It was because she was looking at her shoes. She headed to the car. It wasn't snow but it was something that she walked on. She fumbled with the keys as she opened the door. She leaned forward as she drove. It stilled her shaking hands. When she exhaled it fogged the window. She ran numbers in her head. She planned her money for gas and food like there was someplace that she was driving towards. She was driving towards running out of money. She thought that. She spent some at this liquor store outside a casino. The Gordon's was in a plastic flask. It was in lieu of food. The seal cracked when she unscrewed the cap. She gulped once it hit her lips. It burned her throat and warmed the car. It lit her brain so that she had to squint. The buzz trumped panic. She drank more as she drove. Her thoughts were all shredded. She built this lame logic all piecemeal. *I'll just end up wherever it is that I run out of gas, I'll sell the car and get a job, It'll work out.* Such was her litany. When she reached for the bottle it was lighter by half. Fuck, is what she thought. It was because some spilled on her jeans. It was because the car swerved when she looked down. It was dusk and she was coming through a pass. What light there was barely hit the road. She had to force herself to focus to see. Trees were borne from seams next to streams. She thought *Oh my god.* It was something in the shadows of the branches. The siren accompanied the lights behind her. She couldn't move because stuff was frozen inside her. It was the gin on her breath and in her blood and in the bottle sitting on the seat. She tucked it next to the console. The police car pulled behind her. He said something to her through the window. She said she didn't know. The car wasn't hers and she didn't have a license. That's what she thought, it's why she panicked. She said she was speeding because the car was overheating. He glanced away. She said she was trying to make it to the nearest exit. He asked her for her license and registration. She said it was in her backpack. She said it was in the trunk. He said he'd send someone to help with the car. He walked back towards his. When she kicked the door closed with her knee she was weighted down by her backpack. She ran straight for the shadows. They were shaped like trees. This barbed wire fence cut along these cattails. She hopped it at a post. She ran through slough and bracken. It was the trees she was aiming for. She didn't look back until she hit them. The cars and the cop were a blur against the traffic and the lights behind them. It was a forest 3 yards in. She ran, kept. Her ankle twisted when her foot stuck in the mud. She limped and kept limping. She panted and paused. She had run downhill to get to the spot where the ground just ran away from her. She stood straight against the steep. The rain that pressed her bangs down was snow that melted from the branches that spanned above her. She thought she heard cars and people. It was water rushing, blood ringing in her ears. She swore the lights she saw were traffic, houses. She swore they were safety of some sort. She ran toward them. She was too drunk and it was too dark to see the ground cut off at the wall of the abandoned quarry in front of her. She just fell through the air and towards the water. The lights were the center of her frantic vision. They were just stars coming through the trees but they still looked like a way for her to get the fuck out of there because they just had to.

PART THREE:
REACH FOR THE DEAD

Are you there? The way I am here.
– William Gibson

SPRING

The forest was trees and undergrowth that covered the splay of these mountains that ran towards the horizon in all directions. Hague's body floated in this abandoned quarry hidden all deep in it. These kids were camping on the water's edge. When they called the police they said that it looked like there was a body in the quarry. That's what they said that they saw. What it was that they saw in the rain was black water and mineral walls, a poor and lost kid that'd choked on freezing water until he had drowned. The campers just milled beneath their rain fly. The sun rose behind the trees and clouds. When the kids breathed they saw their breath. This girl said *Maybe it's just,* she paused. She said that she didn't know. The police came with an ambulance. The old logging road they used just went so far. They took it on foot, the trail it became. The space between the trees and the sky and the trees and other trees was the shape of the wind. The sound rushed the way water rushes. The kids met the cops when they came into the clearing. They pointed at the quarry. Hague's body was a shape in the gaining pale. The kids started tearing down their tents because they just wanted to get out of there. The rain ran off their parkas, their sopped gear and brows. This diver piloted a zodiac. EMT's helped him haul Hague's body onto it. The police carried it on a stretcher. The pale flesh left this putrid wake. A cop spat after they wheeled the stretcher into the ambulance. His forehead rested on the open door of his cruiser. He used the ID they recovered from Hague's wallet to ID him. What information he garnered lead him to Karen. She stood there and cried at the bank. It was after she answered her phone. The line went quiet then. It was because she had to put the phone down after what the fuck he had told her. What he had told her was that he was investigating these remains that'd been recovered. He told her that what they had recovered was her son. Karen told him to do what he felt was best. She wrote on her hand with a pen. When she repeated herself it was her sobbing. The cop said that he was *Sorry, so sorry*. The line was dead and she stood there with the phone against her ear. It was dark there in the building then. It was from the trees that surrounded the building. She shook in the chair she'd just sat in. The air was cold from air conditioning. She leaned forward. This woman said something to her. Karen said *I just*. She just took off. It was all dark tile and wood, the lobby she walked through. Her car was hot with the windows up against the sun. She smoked as she drove across town. She sat in her driveway, wrenched her fingers through her hair. The engine was silent beneath the ringing in her ears. She lugged her suitcase out the front door. The car started and Karen sat in it with her hand still turning the key in the ignition. The road lead to a grocery store. Karen sat in the parking lot. She poured blended whiskey from a plastic bottle into an empty can. It splashed onto her lap. She just poured it and kept pouring until the can was brimming. The freeway was a straight line. She got drunk as she drove and she stayed drunk because she kept sipping on the can.

Night turned into darker night against her headlights. She watched the sky tar and mottle. She felt the road gain and sweep. When she reached into the back she grabbed the whiskey bottle from underneath the seat. She undid the cap with her teeth. The whiskey burned in her chest when she breathed. It was 4:30 in the morning when she stopped at a gas station. She bought cigarettes and pills. She held the pump handle as she stole herself against the cold. The horizon was vague and less dark than anything else out there. She just sobbed and drunk drove then. It was so much lighter before she noticed. She pulled off the freeway and over into a parking lot because she had to vomit. Sweat drenched her forehead. She stood with her hands on her knees then she fell to them in the empty parking space next to her car. Her scuffed at skirt peeled off the blood and gravel on the torn knees of her panty hose. She sat there and breathed. She crawled into the driver's seat. Her stomach felt swollen and hard when she lay back. It was pain and cold that woke her up. Karen lit a cigarette and started the car. She bought coffee and a hotdog at a 7-11. She drove heaving for hours then. The motel she found was residential and she ran to her room. She had diarrhea in the toilet. She vomited in the tub. What she heard as she sat on the bathroom tile was someone knocking on her door. She did the chain latch. A man stood in front of the light that filled the space she was staring at. His poncho was a garbage bag. He asked Karen for spare change. He asked her if he could bum a smoke. When he coughed it rattled and he made like to step forward. That's what Karen thought. She just slammed the door and did the deadbolt. The sound was off on the TV in her room because she couldn't get it to work. She sat at the foot of the bed with her slip on over her panties. Blue light filled the room because the TV was the only light in it. The whiskey was a film dried on the inside of the bottle. She tried to pour some down her throat. She tried until she fell asleep. When she drank water in the morning it tasted like her mouth. Sick panic coursed through her breaths as the world came at her open eyes. She swallowed and kept swallowing. The police station was small because the town closest to the quarry was. They led Karen down a hall. She held her shit together. It was because her hangover made everything horrible regardless. She sat in a room. Pine paneling loomed, the door, windows, and paintings.

The cop she'd spoken to gave her papers to sign. He sat down in a chair next to her. When she looked up light came through the window and filled the room. She just shut her eyes against it. The seizure lasted god knows how long. When Karen opened her eyes she stared at the roof of the ambulance she lay in. It moved and she moved with it. Her arms and legs felt numb. She felt something twitch somewhere. She felt the canvas straps that stretched across her chest and thighs as she shook.

The carpet matched the chairs in the waiting room. Karen leaned back in hers. When she licked her teeth she swallowed plaque and lipstick. Her head felt strapped from her jaw and behind her brow. She strained to focus her glassy eyes. An old woman stood in front of her then. The nametag on her sweater said volunteer. The plastic cup she held shook because of her hand. Karen saw ice in it and falling out of it. When the woman said *Dear* she meant Karen. She reached out with her arm and Karen saw it coming at her. It was to show her the ice. The woman told her to hold some of it in her mouth. She said *Even if you can't have water, you can have it.* She said *See?* Karen told her she could have liquids now. *Ok?* The woman said she was sure it would be. Karen thought *What?* Neither of them spoke. The woman said *Whatever it is that ails you.* Karen sat there as the woman walked away. She watched until she couldn't see her. It was that her vision gave way to the distance. She closed her eyes. She pressed her fist to her lips, like it would block what sounds she made as she sobbed.

Karen stood in the exam room. It was all windows across the back. When she peeled the curtains she saw a parking lot. The pane felt warm from the sun because it filled everything she saw. The doctor asked her how long it had been since her diagnosis. Karen turned her head. He asked her to sit down. She thought sentences and spoke words. She shook her head and swung her legs. It marked time like it was divisible. The doctor said *Brain, lung, kidney, liver.* He said that it had spread into her bones. He put his hand on her shoulder. The wall moved toward her because she leaned forward. Karen wrapped her arms around her waist. The doctor looked over the top of his glasses. She was quiet. She just got up. The lights in the hall were brighter than they had been. The floor was a mezzanine. She walked through an atrium. It wasn't scuffs on the elevator doors, it was grease. Karen drank warm water from a rusty fountain. Windows showed a landscaped courtyard. Her anxiety came in waves. She stood in the parking garage. She pulled a cigarette from the pack that she'd pulled from her purse. Her lighter flame wavered until she used both hands. She paced all consternated. She ran through ways for what was true to not be like that was possible. Her ankle twisted when she took this step. She began to fall. She felt something break when she tried to break it. It was all bright then, her pain and everything she saw.

This nurse pushed Karen down a hall in the basement of the hospital. They passed beneath windows set below the ceiling tile. Karen said *We're underground.* The nurse said *Yes honey, we are.* The brick walls were white washed. Karen winced from the glare that came off the floor. It disappeared when they turned this corner. The room the nurse left her in was an office. Her wheelchair rocked back and forth when she tried to get up and out of the chair like getting out of there was something she could just do. Karen just sat there. She saw that she had worn a scrape in the wall paper. This woman walked into the room then. She pressed down the front of her skirt. She held Karen's hand. Karen leaned. To the woman it looked like she was looking through her. She dimmed the light knob because Karen said *The light* when the woman had asked her how she felt. The woman said that she, she breathed, she said *I need you to confirm that you are* foregoing *further treatment.* She paused. *Karen.* Karen nodded. The woman asked her if she had a strategy for ongoing care. She said that in the absence of treatment her conditions could only, her voice cracked and she stopped talking. She told Karen that she was only going to get worse. *How are you going to handle that?* Karen closed her eyes. She told the woman that she wasn't crying. It was her medicine when she slurred. The woman let go of Karen's hands. She watched them fiddle on her lap. She reached for this box of tissues sitting on the desk they were sitting in front of. *Karen, there's this home.* She said that she would forward information regarding her situation. She said that she would recommend her application.

The sun on the mountain was grey and the interior of the ambulance was lit by the dome light because the driver was looking at a map or something. Karen saw him hold the wheel with his knees. They ran over a branch in the road and he pulled the ambulance off and onto the shoulder. Karen sat in the cab as he kneeled by the front bumper. Chill air came in through the vents and off of the windows. She shook beneath her jacket as she stared forward. All she saw through the windshield was shadows and trees smeared by the rain that washed through the forest and over the road. Spray drenched her when the driver opened his door. The road hit these switchbacks. They lead to this meadow. The drive they took was gravel. Coppice as tall as the wheel wells hemmed both sides. The rain stopped and everything that Karen saw was lit by the rose colored light that came in low and from beneath the trees in the distance. The driver parked where the grass had been matted. The facility was house shaped and backlit. The driver put Karen in a wheelchair. He pushed her on a foot path with her leg propped on a bracket. Boards and bricks were steps and he lifted the chair and Karen backwards over them. The sky was blue and orange behind the building. That's what Karen saw. It was this enormous door that they were stopped before. Karen looked like she was staring forward but she was just facing the door. A woman stepped out of it. She said *Hello, Thank you.* She did something to the lock after the driver. The foyer gave way to a hall. The walls were sheetrock panels taped to OSB boards. The woman told Karen she should call her sister. Karen nodded. The nun told her that she needed to apologize for the cold. She said it was the boiler. *There's just the kitchen, and a handful of rooms that can be heated.*

125

Karen didn't know where the nun was when she stood behind the wheelchair. Her neck hurt when she turned. Window light showed dust in the air. Karen watched it hang. She heard the wheelchair wheels against the carpet as the nun and she encroached on the hall.

Karen lay in a bed as lamplight cut at the hoody shadows on the wall behind her. She looked across the room. What light there was that came into the room came in from these French doors. It didn't brighten, it showed. A coffee table stood in front of a couch. The couch sat beneath a mirror. It was a painting. Karen saw that. Her eyes ached from strain. The nun opened the doors and walked outside. She said that the air was good for Karen to breathe. It was thawing ice that her clogs cracked on when she stepped. Karen stared forward. The ground and sky were white from snow and light. The air was cold and thin and she felt it on her face. She clenched her jaw, squinted. The nun rubbed her hands together. Her voice was a backdrop for the headache behind Karen's eyes. Karen hung her head. When she vomited the nun scurried. She lifted the soiled blankets off of her. She grasped Karen's chin as she scrubbed at the puke on her face. The washcloth just smeared it. Something yellow ran down the corners of her mouth. Karen was buzzy and despondent. The hall was a black tunnel. The bathroom was lit and tiled. She ran the faucets in the tub, the nun. Steam filled the room behind the closed door. Karen put her face in her hands as she sat on the toilet. It was the murk that she breathed. She lost her balance when she tried to get up after she pissed. Her right knee bled where the cast on her left leg had abraded it. The nun hauled her up off the floor. She asked her if she was ok. Karen ached all over. She just told her that she was cold. The nun got her into the tub. They were both blind from the steam. The nun braced Karen's cast on the far edge of the tub. She closed the door when she left. Karen held her head above the water. She perspired from her face and from her scalp. Her pulse raced in the heat. When she vomited again it was just bile. She didn't stop because she couldn't. The wretch floated in the water and on the surface. Karen choked as she slid down. She swallowed what crap she was submerged in. She spat when she gasped. Karen heard the nun open the door. She looped her arms beneath Karen's arm pits and pulled her from the mess. Karen lay naked on the floor. The nun stood over her with her hands on her knees. She panted as she wiped Karen's skin in the clearing air. The nun draped her in a robe. Karen limped as she leaned on the nun. She fell back into the wheelchair. The nun helped her onto the couch. Her cast had cracked and begun to unravel. The nun tied it with gauze. She covered Karen with wool blankets. Karen's head pounded. She sucked on her parched gums and aching teeth. Her eyes were less scopes than walls and it was the world that smashed against them. Bruises formed on her face and hands. The nun had her swallow tablets. The light in the room began to etch and flake. The skin around Karen's eyes became scabbed and inflamed. She stared out the window set in the wall across from her. She saw through the snow to where there was no snow. Karen winced. The nun injected Karen's belly with a syringe. The nun said it was saline. Karen felt fluid in her stomach. She was wracked by coughs then. Acid burned her throat and her nostrils. *I'm going to die tomorrow.* Everything outside the window was snow flocked. Karen stared until she couldn't see because it was invisible. Time passed. Karen blinked. What light there was in the room pulsed in time with her pulse. It hastened, faded. The window was just a black panel then.

Karen said that her son had gone to find her daughter. She told the nun that Tuesday had stolen her housemate's car then vanished when the police tried to arrest her. She'd fled on foot, disappeared into these woods. That's what they told Karen and that's what she told the nun. She told the nun it was the same woods that Hague said he was camping in when he called her after having taken a bus across the state. Karen's handkerchief was a paper towel. She soaked it with bile when she coughed. The yellow tray she rested her elbows on looked green the way her skin just looked so pale. When she said *They* she meant these kids. She said they were camping in the same woods where Hague was, that they found his body floating in this lake. Her nose ran onto her trembling lips. The nun knelt in front of her and wiped them. She hugged her then held her. Karen sobbed as she muttered. She said the police told her that there was a landslide, that it was an accident and it just happened. The nun let go of her and sat back on her feet. Karen said that it didn't matter what anyone told her. *What happened was that Hague had gone to tell Tuesday that I was dying but he died instead.* She said she was sure that Tuesday was dead anyway so the whole thing was just fucked right from the start. *I told Haguey. I told him that the police said her trail was dead so they were sure she was.* Her throat sounded hoarse when she spoke. It just ached no matter how much water she sipped on. She told the nun that none of this would have happened if she had told Tuesday herself. *I had called her then. Tuesday. We arranged to meet. I was going to tell her that I had cancer.* What happened was that their conversation fell apart right from the first. That's what Karen said. She told the nun that the last time she saw Tuesday she was sitting at a picnic table screaming as Tuesday ran past the restaurants on the side street that ran away from the park where they had met.

Karen said that Tuesday found Engles. She meant her husband after he killed himself. *The kids were children. Engles had been taking medicine. It stopped working when he stopped taking it. I had no clue. I walked into the bedroom and saw Tuesday kneeling by him. My eyes screwed against the light like it was too bright but it was too dark. I walked then stood. The drapes were drawn. I saw that and all these shadows. All that I saw was this crumpled mess. I didn't know what I saw. Pieces of the ceiling must have torn away from the studs when the ceiling fan had ripped away beneath Engles' weight. It wasn't supposed to be there. I knelt when I fell to my knees. I tried grabbing at the belt around his neck like it would undo what he had done. Blood blisters had formed beneath the buckle. I couldn't work it. Twos was so smart. We heard Hague come home and open the front door. She got the kid in his room and locked him in it. He knew there was something going on but he didn't know what thank you jesus fucking christ. He wailed and pounded on his door. That's what I heard when I called 911. I rested my forehead in my palm. When the ambulance arrived they didn't shut the siren off. I had to leave Engles to let them in. I stood in the hall with my arm around Tuesday. I closed my eyes or my sobbing did something to them. Light flashing and my crying came in waves in time with the siren. The EMT's carried Engles on a stretcher. I lead them to the front door like they needed to know how to find it. I rested my hand on the sheet on Engles' chest until they lifted him into the back of the ambulance. It was so loud, the siren. I got in the car to follow them to the hospital. It was quiet then.*

Karen spoke to Hague as she held him as they lay beneath the covers of his bed. She said *Your dad's not here. He's dead Hague.* It was because the kid had woken up screaming for his father. He sobbed and so did Karen. His tears ran into her hair. He dribbled spit and sputum. *Haguey Haguey Hague.* It didn't matter how tightly she held him, things would still fall apart. She knew that.

He pressed his face against her chest. It was a different blackness he saw than the blackness he saw behind his lids when he shut them. Karen thought that. She thought that was different from the blackness she saw when she stared across the room.

It was days and then a week. It came on a month. The nun took Karen out on the grounds. They were in a patch covered with ice-covered snow. The nun gestured. She told Karen there had been a grove. She said that there had been this fire. One of the trees was struck by lightning and it spread. That's what the nun said. They were in front of the charred remains of an outbuilding then. Karen leaned and reached. She touched at the wood propped against a board. It was just frozen ash and it crumpled. The nun exhaled and her breath just hung there. The sky was orange and pink. It dulled to something star smattered. Karen thought it was afternoon. She thought that there was no way that it could ever end. The path back was wheelchair tracks that they backtracked over. Because of the trees and the building there wasn't any place she could see where the light touched the ground. It just kept getting darker and colder. Inside the nun left Karen bundled. Pills stopped her chills and dulled her pain. The nun didn't leave the room because she didn't want to leave Karen alone because she didn't want her to die alone. Karen's seizure was just a pause in her not moving. She breathed through the corner of her mouth. She slurred when she opened it. The nun told her that the room smelled like crap because that's what she had done. She felt the crook of Karen's neck with her chapped hand. She began to undress her. Karen struck rigid poses. Her eyes spun behind flicking lids. The nun pressed down her shoulders to hold her flat. She jammed her fingers into Karen's mouth. She panted when she rolled off of her. The nun got up. Her knees and smock were smeared with blood because that's what was pouring out of Karen then. The nun ran across the room and picked up the handset off the telephone. She watched a stain pool and widen beneath Karen. She clicked the hook switch on the phone. She kept. It was because there was no way she could know the lines were down. She dropped the receiver. Karen lay on the floor. The nun put pillows beneath her head and piled blankets on her. She started to cry because she couldn't help it. The car was in the garage 60 yards away from the facility. The nun pulled her coat hood on. The thing hung off her like a cape. Her eyes burned. It was the cold. She felt it on her skin and when she swallowed. It was her running to the car and everything.

PART FOUR:
SPEM IN ALIUM

Thought, which is matter, cannot seek that which is beyond time, for thought is memory, and the experience in that memory is as dead as the leaf of last autumn.
– J. Krishnamurti

The rain formed puddles. Tuesday ran through them as she ran through the motel parking lot. Her socks and jean cuffs were soaked. She pounded the office door with her fist and palm. She told the manager that she was looking for her mother. She kept talking and she didn't stop. The man looked at her. He pulled his pants up over his gut. She told him that she didn't know what room she was in. The man asked her how long she had lived here. *Months, maybe more.* She begged him *Please*. He told her it could only be a couple rooms. Tuesday pushed open this door he unlocked. She saw this girl sit on a bed as a bearded man leaned over her arm and pushed a syringe into her elbow crook. Tuesday stepped backwards and the girl looked up dazed all suddenly. The man stared intent on her arm and the syringe. Tuesday slammed the door and she dashed down the landing. The man from the office followed her. He stopped her. The door they tried just opened because it wasn't locked. What Tuesday saw was Karen struck like the floor was something she was leaning against. Her skin showed pale in the room's caviness. It was the pool of blood forming beneath her. Such was the bullshit Tuesday saw sprawled there. The manager asked Tuesday what the fuck was going on. Tuesday didn't know her mother had this tumor. She knew she was hemorrhaging. It was plain as fucking day, she thought. She didn't say anything. The manager said that he was going to get help. Tuesday lay down next to Karen and held her. The blood coming out of her vagina had begun to clot in her skirt and on her thighs. Karen had this stare and Tuesday stared into it. Something happened outside the door then. Someone pounded on it. *Mom, Mom, Mom, I love you, I love you, I love you.* Karen wasn't breathing. The door opened. It let in people and light. Tuesday didn't let go of her mother as she lay there. She was covered in the whatever then, the cancerous blood.